Shattered by Secrets

Laws of Passion, Volume 1

Amara Holt

Published by Amara Holt, 2024.

Copyright © 2024 by Amara Holt

All rights reserved.

No part of this book may be reproduced, distributed, or transmitted in any form or by any means, including photocopying, recording, or other electronic or mechanical methods, without the prior written permission of the author, except in the case of brief quotations in book reviews.

This is a work of fiction. Names, characters, places, and incidents are the product of the author's imagination or are used fictitiously. Any resemblance to actual events, organizations, locales, or persons, living or dead is coincidental and is not intended by the authors.

PROLOGUE

Zachary

17 YEARS OLD

The cars moved through the crowd of people. I was alone, while my parents and little sister were in the car ahead of us.

Scarlett was going through a terrible phase, often even the nanny struggled to manage the little one.

The thousands of American flags fluttered tirelessly. My eyes were captivated by it all—the posters, the thousands of signs, the image of my father.

The new President of America. I witnessed how he barely slept over the past year, with so many tasks and countless commitments. As Scarlett would say, *"a total madhouse."*

But if there was one thing I learned, it's that dedication, coupled with good performance, yields its rewards. Even though my father barely had a moment to himself, he made a lot of time for us and was dedicated until the very last day, the day of the final vote. We were anxious, with all the family gathered at our house in California.

The only voice we heard was Scarlett's, always impatient, asking if we were okay because we all remained silent.

Then the results came in, and Arnold Fitzgerald was elected the new President of the United States.

I couldn't even celebrate. I only allowed myself to collapse onto the sofa and let out a long sigh of relief. It was all worth it, all the times we had to accompany my father—it was worth it.

It was my last year of school, and I couldn't even attend. Private tutors were hired to accompany us on the campaign trips with Dad.

Many said this couldn't be called a life, but I argued it was quite the opposite. It was exactly what I wanted. Growing up in a prominent political family made me just as addicted.

This was where I wanted to be, in politics, doing what the Fitzgeralds did best—governing all of America.

The cars slowed down, stopping in front of that enormous monument, *the White House.*

My door was opened, as were all the others. My uncles, who were part of my father's party, were there as well.

All the men of power were present for his inauguration.

It felt like everything was moving in slow motion as I turned my face, seeing Dad waving to the voters. The applause and cheers followed; he was being hailed. Everyone wanted him as President.

This was what I wanted, all those applause, being in power, knowing every step by heart, *"front to back," "back to front."* I grew up watching my grandfather in power, then my father. My uncles were in the same sphere. I lived and breathed politics, knowing that one day this would be my future.

CHAPTER ONE

Savannah

Years Later...

At that moment, my life could have been the song *"Breathless"* – *The Corrs*. I was finally in California, just a dreamer girl starting a new life. I left everything *behind*; that girl was gone. I wasn't going to let fear take over me; shyness would no longer be a part of this new woman.

I was no longer a girl; now I was a 22-year-old woman.

I felt like I was in a movie, with the music in my headphones making me swear I could see people dancing to its rhythm. *I was probably going crazy at that moment.*

I had left my truck at Auntie's house just to breathe in the California atmosphere, so different from Arizona.

It must have been in my head, but everything felt different. A dreamer's mind sometimes makes the world seem pink, my favorite color.

I didn't know anything about Sacramento. Auntie said not to go out alone; she would come with me after work. But anxiety got the better of me, and here I was, smiling at any stranger passing by.

Just a girl from Arizona in California.

I lifted my face, opened my arms, spinning around, closed my eyes, wanting to scream but holding back. I smiled widely. The childhood dream of living in California with my aunt.

It took Dad a long time to let me go; after all, in his mind, his little girls shouldn't leave his care. But with Mom's help, I managed it. Here I was. Of course, my mother didn't want me to leave Arizona either, but I wanted to be here. I needed to spread my own wings, to be a little bird ready to fly.

It took a lot of courage, and that's what I had. Or so I thought.

I bumped into someone, my arms tangled in something. I opened my eyes to see the irritated eyes of a woman. I apologized, but she didn't respond, merely sighed and continued walking, looking annoyed.

Well, her bad mood wasn't going to ruin my first outing in Sacramento.

Maybe I shouldn't have been spinning around on a busy street. I started walking again, lost in my music.

My lively steps led me to a street. I looked only one way; perhaps the excitement made me inattentive.

I touched my boot on the asphalt and started taking one step at a time.

That abrupt movement next to me made me turn my face quickly. Startled, I let out a scream as the front of a car threw me back, causing me to fall.

The headphones fell from my ears, the lively music replaced by that dramatic moment. After scraping my knees on the ground, I landed on my backside, with people gathering around me.

Damn, maybe my life wasn't a romance movie but rather an emotionless drama.

A groan escaped my mouth amid the pain from my scraped knees.

"Miss?" That male voice made me turn my face in shock. "Are you hurt?"

The man with brown hair didn't look at me; he had his head bowed to my knees. His outfit was nothing less than a suit. Such a man didn't fit into my life. I had never even seen one of those suited and booted guys in person.

"I don't think it's anything serious, just a few scratches," I muttered, reaching for my knee. It seemed the man tried to do the same, causing our fingers to touch briefly. A sudden shock ran through my body, and I pulled my hand away.

The stranger lifted his eyes, leaving me amazed by his striking features.

"I need to get you out of here," he said, not breaking eye contact.

"Believe me, sir, it's nothing," I declared, knowing that a minor scrape on my knees wouldn't ruin my day.

Maybe that man's blue eyes had the power to dominate my mind. I touched my hand to the asphalt and noticed a flash coming our way. I looked back at the stranger as he seemed to scowl at the flash. After all, who was he? *I was sure he was extraordinarily handsome, but I didn't remember him being any Hollywood star.*

"Even if it's nothing, it's my duty to help you." I jumped when he expertly grasped both my shoulders, helping me to my feet with such ease it felt like I weighed half a pound.

"Uh..." I mumbled as I stood up. "It didn't seem to hurt when I was sitting."

I grimaced, seeing a small trail of blood trickling down my knee and leg.

"Damn, I hate blood." I looked around, wondering if any passerby had a tissue to spare.

"Come on, miss, I'll get you out of here." He placed a hand on my shoulder, acting like he was my father.

"Sir, I'm fine." How could I get into someone's car that I didn't know?

I looked down for my headphones and saw one of them near the sewer drain.

"Damn, no." I whimpered, realizing that the other one had fallen inside.

"Come on, miss, we need to get out of here before we make a headline," he grumbled impatiently.

"After all, who are you? Who are those men taking pictures of you?" I turned my face away, lost in my pink world, more concerned about my headphone than about the stranger or my scraped leg.

"You really don't know who I am?" His blue eyes widened subtly.

"If I knew, I wouldn't be calling you 'sir,'" I retorted, trying to pull my arm away to go look for my headphone in the sewer. With some luck, I might get it back.

"Damn it, what are you staring at the sewer for?" he whispered as if not wanting us to be overheard.

"My headphone fell in there," I stated the obvious.

"That's probably why you were distracted. Come on, miss, I'll get you as many headphones as you want, but for God's sake, come with me." I lifted my face.

With his well-groomed beard, incredibly handsome face, blue eyes, and the perfectly tailored suit, he didn't seem like someone who would take advantage of an insignificant girl like me. I let out a long sigh.

"Fine, you owe me a headphone," I replied, letting him pull me by the elbow.

Who was this man, after all? We hadn't even introduced ourselves; he didn't care to know my name. He must have been someone important, considering he had two shiny black cars. The back door was opened, he entered first, and I followed last, noticing he even had a driver.

This was definitely way beyond my reality.

CHAPTER TWO

Savannah

With the car moving, my eyes turned to the man beside me, who was fiddling with his phone, not even bothering to tell me where we were headed.

"Hey, can you tell me where we're going?" I asked since I wasn't getting any response from him.

For a few seconds, he continued to focus on his phone until I let out a long sigh, which made him look at me.

"We're going to my apartment; we need to clean that wound..."

"I'm not going to your place; I don't know you. I've already said I'm fine, it's nothing," I grumbled, twisting my lip as I looked at my still-stinging knee.

"Seriously, you don't know who I am?"

"You talk as if I'm supposed to know who you are." I gestured with my hand, looking out the window and contemplating the possibility of jumping out of the moving car.

If only I had my truck, I could use the gun I always keep under the seat. One of the things my dad practically forced my sister and me to learn was how to shoot; we're Arizona girls, and we know how to defend ourselves.

"For a while, I thought you were pretending since most women do that to get attention. How can someone be so inattentive and jump in front of a moving car? Do you realize the danger you put yourself in?" His voice was deep, almost irritated.

"I was distracted; people get distracted." I shrugged my shoulders.

"Your distraction could have led to your death." When he said that, I looked at my knees, making a grimace.

"I think this wound is far from killing me." I furrowed my brow, looking back at the stranger.

He rolled his eyes, very close to losing his patience.

"Don't take it literally; I'm saying that if I'd been driving faster, I could have injured you more seriously."

"Thinking that way, it's good that you weren't going fast." I shrugged again. "Seriously, sir, I'm fine. Just drop me off at any corner. This was supposed to be my day, and now I'm in a stranger's car, not knowing where the hell I am in Sacramento. My aunt will be mad for me going out without her since I got distracted..."

"What do you mean, your day?" At that moment, he seemed interested.

"Well, I arrived in Sacramento yesterday. My aunt said I should rest in the morning and that in the afternoon, she'd take me around the city. But as you can see, I didn't rest; maybe I should have. I'm too scared to jump out of a moving car, which is probably why I'm here talking too much about my insignificant life."

"Where in Arizona are you from?" He asked quickly.

"How do you know I'm from Arizona?" I was somewhat startled by that realization.

"Your accent. Californians don't speak like that." I frowned.

"I'm from Marana..."

"Was the flight tiring?" He started asking a new question before I even finished my answer.

"I drove my truck." I replied calmly.

"In a truck? That's hours of travel..."

"Well, it took about fifteen hours. I took a nap at a gas station, made friends with a trucker, and he let me have breakfast with him." I continued nonchalantly.

"With a trucker? You're scared to be in this car with me, but having breakfast with a stranger doesn't bother you?"

"Actually, I knew his name was Joseph, he had three daughters, and his wife is a teacher. I don't know anything about you, except you seem like some kind of god because those flashes surely weren't for me." He frowned, as if looking for some sign of dishonesty.

"Seriously, you're not joking, are you?" He asked again, just as before.

"Should I be suspicious for not knowing your name too? Is that how you Californians are? Suspicious of someone not knowing who you are? You know, in Arizona, people usually introduce themselves." I gave a mocking smile.

"I noticed you don't take any conversation seriously..."

"I noticed you must have had a king's breakfast, which is why you're acting like one," I cut him off.

At that moment, the man gave a brief smile, a small one, pulling his lips to the side, his dark brown hair matching his well-groomed beard.

"My name is Savannah Bellingham, and yours? I believe our conversation could become much less awkward if you tell me your name." I extended my hand.

I waited for him to do the same, and he did, extending his hand and showing off a gold watch on his wrist, which certainly didn't look like the second-hand items sold near my home.

"Zachary Fitzgerald." His hand covered mine, making it seem small in comparison.

"Should I recognize you by your name?" I asked, not letting go of his hand.

"Maybe by my last name, but after this conversation, I believe I've played the king, and there's no way you'd know me..."

"Wait," I cut him off. "I want to see if I can recall something."

With my other hand, I stopped him. Without taking my eyes off him, I bit the corner of my lip, Fitzgerald. I was sure I'd heard that last name at some point in my life. Zachary's blue eyes dropped to my lips, and for some reason, it gave me that delightful tingling I felt with his hand on mine.

"Of course." I broke into a big smile. "I'm not as bad with names as it seems. Fitzgerald, my dad will be floored when he finds out I was with you, but wait, you're too young to have been our president, *no...* you can't be him. After all, his name was Arnold... my head is spinning right now."

Zachary flashed a broad smile, showing off his perfectly aligned white teeth.

"Arnold is my father. I'm the senator of our state." I raised my hand to close my open mouth.

"You can't send me to prison for almost jumping in front of your car, for arguing with you... *oh, heavens,* is this the moment I start begging for mercy? I'm only 22, just starting out in life..."

"Calm down, have they told you that once you start talking, you never stop? And look, we've only known each other for less than an hour. No one's going to jail; you can breathe now."

He even noticed that I was holding my breath. I let it out at that moment, now knowing who the man next to me was. Without a doubt, this would be the craziest story I'd ever be able to tell my future kids.

My first day in California, and what are the chances of jumping in front of the car of one of the men with the most powerful families in our country? I don't understand politics, but I remember Dad always talking about that last name when he spoke with Mom or a neighbor.

I should have been more interested; then I could have made conversation with that handsome man beside me. But in my mind, when Dad mentioned Fitzgerald, all I pictured was some old, fat guy, not the Greek god sitting next to me.

CHAPTER THREE

Savannah

The car entered an underground garage, and my eyes scanned everything around me. I held one hand over the other, becoming anxious about being in that place alone with a man who, while apparently well-known, I did not know at all.

"Have you gone silent, Miss Bellingham?" Zachary's deep voice echoed beside me.

I turned my face, meeting his eyes in the dim light of the vehicle. The illumination was weak in the dark parking area.

"I can still get out of here, Zach. This isn't a good idea. Being alone with you in your apartment means being alone with you. I've never been alone with a man before," I said calmly, nervously rubbing one hand over the other.

"Since you gave me the nickname, I'll call you by your first name. Savannah, I'll clean your wound. I don't want my name in the headlines as the driver who hit a young girl and didn't provide assistance," he said with a solicitous tone.

"Couldn't you have helped by taking me to an emergency room?" I raised a confused eyebrow.

"I don't think this is an emergency room case. We can handle this quickly at my apartment." The car stopped in one of the parking spaces.

My door was opened, as was Zachary's. I took the hand of his security guard, turning my face to see that Zachary was already by my side.

"Let me help you." He extended his hand, and I tentatively took it.

"Senator?" One of the guards called to him. When he turned his face, the man continued, "Is there anything else you need?"

"Stay here. Miss Bellingham will be coming down shortly, and you'll take her home." The guard simply nodded in agreement.

Zachary didn't release my elbow, helping me walk to the elevator.

The doors opened, and we stepped inside. I watched him press the top button. My knees still burned, so I reached into my back pocket and pulled out my phone.

"Oh no," I muttered, disheartened to see that the screen was completely shattered. "*Shit, shit, shit...*"

"What happened?" Zachary looked at me with concern.

"My phone. My butt must have smashed the screen on impact," I complained, not realizing how strange that sentence must have sounded.

I looked up, my eyes widening. Zachary didn't say anything; he was impeccably dressed, with an upright posture, always evaluating. As for me, I had no poise to present myself in front of a government official.

"*Wow*, you must think I'm crazy. My dad always says my sister and I inherited all of our mother's lack of filter, especially when I'm nervous... *shit*, here I am talking too much." I lowered my face, embarrassed.

"Well, it's been a long time since I've had a conversation with the word *shit* repeated so many times. And now we should discuss how strong your butt is to crack a phone screen?" Zachary had a hint of mockery in his expression.

"That's what happens when I talk too much. I deserve your mockery." I felt my cheeks warm up.

The numbers on the display stopped scrolling, halting at the top floor. The doors opened, and Zachary held them open with his hand, motioning for me to walk out.

"Standing still makes my legs hurt more when I start walking," I complained, passing by him.

In the small hallway, there was only one door. Zachary quickly entered a code, unlocking the way.

"Ladies first." He gestured for me to enter.

Without saying anything, a whistle escaped my lips.

"*Wow*, this place is probably the most beautiful I've ever seen." My voice came out as a whisper of admiration.

"Sit on the couch; I'll get the first aid kit." He pointed toward the living room.

I followed where he pointed, the pain in my knee even fading from my mind as my attention was absorbed by the environment. The couch was in light tones, and the entire wall was glass, revealing the city below.

I stopped in front of the glass wall, my fingers touching it. It must be incredible to be a millionaire, to have all those luxuries. Something completely out of my reality.

Maybe the day hadn't turned out so bad after all. When would I ever dream of seeing a penthouse like this?

"Savannah, please, have a seat on the couch." I turned my face to find Zachary now without his polished suit jacket, wearing only his button-down shirt. He had even removed his tie.

"*Ah*, yes." I nodded and walked toward the couch.

In his hands was a small case. I settled onto the upholstered seat.

"Your apartment is beautiful," I complimented.

"Thank you, it's not every day that it gets complimented." He knelt in front of me.

"Sorry, I forgot to take off my boots," I whispered, noticing that he was in shoes, but unlike mine, his were so polished I could almost see my reflection.

"I didn't take mine off. Why should you take yours off?" He seemed to find it amusing.

"It doesn't even compare." I shook my head.

"Stop fussing." He opened his case.

He pulled out a liquid, the label unreadable, and used a gauze to apply it to my knee.

"Ouch!" I winced.

"It's just cold. It won't hurt," he said without looking at me.

"Of course, because it's not on you," I retorted.

Zachary's blue eyes lifted to meet mine, not moving his face, as if he just wanted to see my reaction.

"I thought you'd be tougher," he gently mocked.

"Your assumptions are mistaken." When I saw he was about to clean the other knee, I reached out and grabbed his wrist. "Wait."

"What's the problem?" Zachary seemed amused.

"I said wait." I closed my eyes, counting to ten without letting go of his hand.

"Savannah, is everything okay?" he asked when I opened my eyes.

"I'm just preparing myself. You didn't prepare me for the other knee, so I want to be ready." I started to slowly breathe in and out.

"Savannah, it's just saline." I widened my eyes, meeting his gaze.

"It's not just saline; it's very, very cold saline." I pouted as he quickly moved his hand to my other dirty knee. "Zachary!"

The man broke into a charming smile.

"It's better without preparation." I squinted my eyes tightly against the sting.

I waited for him to finish, noticing that Zachary was applying an ointment. His finger touching my skin sent small shivers through my body.

"Is it over?" I asked with my eyes still closed, hearing the case being closed.

"I don't know, open your eyes and see." I opened one eye, looking around for him, but he was no longer in the room.

Slowly, I opened the other eye. Zachary was no longer in the room. My eyes focused on my knee; there was no more blood, and even the trail of blood that had dripped was cleaned up.

On top was the ointment he had applied. He had taken care of me as he promised.

CHAPTER FOUR

Zachary

Let the girl go, Zach, let her go...
My mind was screaming at me constantly, ever since she got into my car. *Drop her off at any corner*, anywhere out of sight, away from any sensationalist photographers.

But I couldn't do it. I brought that girl up to my penthouse, knowing the risks. I brought her, even though tomorrow was my wedding.

The sensible choice would be to send her home now. Instead, it seemed like I had only helped the poor young woman I had accidentally run over. There's still time to not screw things up.

My phone kept vibrating in my pocket. I knew it was my assistant. He wanted to know what happened; obviously, the accident had reached his ears.

I couldn't be the first to tarnish my family's image. Even though my marriage wasn't for the right reasons, if we're talking about love, Hanna was an old friend. She proposed the union. My friend got involved with a man she didn't even know, got pregnant, and, not wanting to tell her parents, asked me to marry her.

It seemed like a sensible choice to marry her. It gave me the best of both worlds—a marriage in the eyes of my constituents, perfect. We were good friends, we had a lovely friendship, and I could easily accept her child as my own. I didn't care that it wasn't biological.

And on top of that, I could have any woman I wanted in my bed, all agreed upon in a deal.

Hanna was the one who proposed it, and I just agreed.

I wanted to be like my father, but I didn't want a family like his. Not that I didn't like it—I loved my family, unconditionally. But I didn't feel ready to be the man for just one woman.

Send the little girl from Arizona on her way...

My mind alerted me again when I heard the sound of boots entering my kitchen, where I was putting away the first aid kit.

I straightened my back and looked at the anxious and curious blue eyes of the most beautiful woman I had ever seen in front of me.

"I think that's all." She bit the corner of her full lips absentmindedly, her long blonde hair loose on her back. The only thing missing from her *cowgirl* look was a hat.

Women like that usually didn't attract me, but she was proving otherwise, showing me how much I wanted to feel my hands on her curves.

"Are you feeling better?" I asked, holding onto the edge of the island, putting all my willpower into not moving toward her.

"Theoretically, it was just a fall." She shrugged, avoiding my gaze and looking around. She had an incredible curiosity, always observing everything.

Savannah was wearing denim shorts with frayed edges, revealing her legs and making me wonder what it would be like to have my hand there. The tank top had a square neckline, covering her breasts, not even giving me a clear view of their size.

"Could you get me a glass of water?" she asked, nervously.

"What kind of host would I be if I didn't offer a glass of water?" I gave a half-smile and headed toward the fridge.

I opened it, grabbing the pitcher and setting it in the center of the island. Savannah took small steps, my eyes following her fingers as they brushed over the marble. I grabbed a glass from the holder, filled it, and extended it to her.

Delicately, Savannah's fingers took the glass, bringing it to her lips. It made me forget the rest of the world and get lost in the bubble that was Savannah Bellingham. I couldn't shift my focus; even the way she swallowed the liquid fascinated me.

"Is everything okay, Zach?" she asked informally, moistening her lips with the water that made her mouth more hydrated.

I hated being called by my nickname by those not in my family, but that woman, at that moment, could call me whatever she wanted, and it wouldn't make me the least bit annoyed with her.

"Couldn't be better." My voice came out rougher than I expected.

I'm a damned pervert for wanting an innocent young woman. It's clear in every look of hers, every reaction, even when I touched her to clean the wound. Savannah shivered, blushed numerous times; she is innocent. She doesn't deserve to be defiled by someone like me. All I want is just sex, a good, intense fuck, and then she can go away, disappear from my life.

Tomorrow, I'm getting married—married to my best friend, a marriage that I can't even call a marriage because I don't love her the way a husband and wife should. To me, Hanna is just a friend. That's all, and that's how she sees me too.

"Thanks for the water." She walked to the sink, where I saw her turn on the tap, rinsing the glass and setting it by the sink.

Rubbing her hand over her denim shorts, she turned back to face me.

"You should go now, Miss Bellingham," I declared without moving, trying to make the most sensible decision because it could take me a few more minutes to change my mind.

"Oh, yes," for some reason, the way I spoke seemed to sadden her. She lowered her face, her blonde hair falling over her shoulders.

I liked her talkative version. But I shouldn't like that; Savannah was just the girl from Arizona I ran over, that's all. Tomorrow, she would be nothing more; tomorrow, I would have forgotten her.

"I'll walk you to the door." I finally remembered how to speak again, heading toward the door of my penthouse, hearing the young woman's footsteps right behind me.

I turned when I stopped in front of the door. She was right behind me, distracted, stopping and standing in front of me. Savannah was a petite woman; I could easily hold her close, but she would never be the ideal woman to be by my side. She was too sweet and naive; my world would eat her alive.

"Thank you for taking care of the wound," I instinctively noticed she took a step toward me, standing on the tips of her toes.

In a ridiculous reaction, I took a step back, making Savannah immediately blush.

"Oh, I'm sorry. I'm just used to saying goodbye with a kiss on the cheek, *I... I...*" she bit her lip, embarrassed.

I wanted to be the one biting those lips. It should be me.

"It's fine. It was just an impulsive move on my part." This time, I took a step closer, lowered my face, and with her lips so close to mine, I said, "You know what, fuck it..."

CHAPTER FIVE

Savannah

His whisper was like a fuse inside me, leaving me completely on fire. Zachary's strong hands pushed me against the wall next to us, his mouth taking mine. It was the first time a man of his stature had kissed me.

I had kissed other men, flirted, and more, but none had made me want to lose my virginity. It wasn't something I saved for marriage; I just wanted it to be with someone who made my legs go weak, making me forget everything else in the world.

His lips fit against mine, his tongue finding its way in, *oh God...* Zachary kissed with his tongue, it was magical, feeling it entwine with mine, an urgent kiss, his body pressing against mine. I raised my hands, wanting to touch his shoulder.

Seemingly having anticipated my action, he released my face, stepped back, and held both my wrists above my head, pressing them against the wall.

"Don't touch me." His voice was rough, laden with pleasure.

"But why?" I whispered, not understanding, searching for my breath that I had lost somewhere.

"I'm not touched during sex, or at any intimate moment with a woman...

"I don't understand," I said again, still confused.

"Savannah, sweet and lovely girl from Arizona, your lips just proved what I knew, you're deliciously sweet." With his other hand, he traced my lips. "I'm not touched, I don't have sex with touches, only I can touch you."

"I'm sorry, Zachary, but why is that?" I murmured, parting my lips, letting my breath escape desperately.

"Only one woman has touched me in my entire life, and I fell in love with her, unconditionally, but she wasn't fit to be by my side. She couldn't keep up with my fast-paced life. She wanted me to be by her side at all times, but my work will always come first, which is why she left me. I suffered for a love I couldn't have, and at that moment, I decided no other woman would touch me. If you want to have sex with me, it has to be on my terms." He removed his hand from my face, pulled out his tie from his pocket, and held it up.

I stared at it for a long moment. The senator was offering me sex. That wasn't me; I didn't have sex with a man I had just met, who wouldn't even let me touch him.

It was clear that Zachary wanted sex, he wanted me, but it would be just a fleeting encounter for him.

"I... I..." I tried to speak, but nothing came out.

"*Sweetie,* that's all you'll get from me, sex. There's no possibility of anything else." He whispered, as if trying to get that tie onto my wrist.

What were the chances of something like this happening to a girl from Arizona? I promised myself I wouldn't let my shyness take over. And what bigger madness could I commit? It would make for a story.

I would finally have something to say about myself that wasn't so tame and boring, though it wasn't something I'd be able to discuss with just anyone, since sex wasn't a topic for friendly chats.

I figured just saying I was run over by the Senator from California was a good story. I should refuse, it was too much madness, the kind of thing Savannah Bellingham didn't do. I could hear Cindy Murphy's voice yelling at me, *you coward, you coward.* Cindy always had the power to make me embarrass myself in front of the whole school, and it seemed she still had that power in my mind.

"Savannah?" Zachary pulled me out of my reverie.

"I'm a virgin," I said as if that could be enough for Zachary to open his door and send me away, so I wouldn't be the one to say no. I couldn't take the blame for refusing to be in his sheets, which I bet were as expensive as everything else about him screamed millionaire.

"Is that a problem?" Zachary said, as he tied the tie around my wrist, not stopping him, letting him secure it there.

Maybe I should just let myself be carried away by the tension of the moment.

"I'm not as experienced as the women you must be used to," I felt my face heat up, raising my face, noticing that the senator had tied a knot so tight around my wrist that it was impossible to undo.

"I'm not demanding," he whispered, his eyes fixed on me.

"Let me touch you, you won't fall in love with me." I pouted, realizing the senator had a brief smile.

"*Sweetie*, the most innocent ones are the most dangerous. We shouldn't be here, we shouldn't be about to do what we both want, but I still want to, I need to feel your body, I need to know what sounds that little mouth of yours can make." His hands were now fully at my mercy, while mine were restrained by the tie.

"It's not fair, it's my first time, and I have to be tied up? I just wanted to feel you, Zach, just like you're going to feel me." I closed my eyes as the senator's face moved to the curve of my neck, leaving delicious kisses that made me shiver.

"That's my condition. Do you accept, Savannah? I'm willing to take your virginity, but you need to know that tomorrow, everything will be forgotten, we won't see each other again, you'll be just another one in my life," he whispered, making me even more tense.

I should refuse, I shouldn't accept, but of all the madness I could commit, maybe this was by far my freedom, it would prove to me that I was no longer the foolish girl from Arizona.

"Am I the first girl you're taking virginity from?" I asked, seeing his eyes meet mine.

"Yes," he whispered, dragging his beard along my cheek.

"Then promise me I'll always be the first? That there won't be another? That way I won't feel so insignificant for losing my virginity to a man I'll never see again," I begged, my voice breathless.

Zachary looked deeply into my eyes, his intense blue eyes as if they could pierce my soul.

"I promise, sweet Savannah," I believed the senator's promise, closing my eyes as his lips touched mine.

CHAPTER SIX

Savannah

Zachary grabbed the hem of my shirt, his eyes fixed on my belly, which was starting to show, and I felt the slight chill of the ambient air touching my skin.

"Looks like you'll need to remove the tie," I whispered, trying to find a way for him to release it.

"Your attempt won't work with me," he murmured, pulling the shirt over my head.

The fabric stopped at my elbows.

"Another thing keeping my arms up." I pouted a bit.

"That won't even be a problem..." A little squeal escaped my mouth when he lifted me into his arms.

His hand gripping my butt over the jeans of my shorts. My face was close to the senator's, our eyes locked; there was no way to look away, as if the entire coverage could be impregnated by the tension of our bodies.

He walked with me in his arms, one of his hands sliding along my back. As we passed through the living room, I realized this wouldn't be where we'd have our encounter. My curious eyes quickly surveyed the entire room as we entered.

"I don't know why I'm still surprised," I whispered with a groan.

He laid me down in the center of the bed, the soft mattress welcoming me as if with open arms.

"Any problems, Arizona girl?" My arms were above my head, the senator's hands touching my belly, his face coming closer along with his hand. I felt his beard brushing against me, leaving slow, soft kisses, making me shiver all over.

"My tied-up hands are a big problem when I'm at a disadvantage," I whispered, rolling my eyes and biting the corner of my lip.

"No, sweet Savannah, if I let you go, there might be something of me you don't want," he said as if it were a grave mistake.

"At this moment, I want everything from you, Senator." Zachary lifted his eyes to me.

It was as if what I said touched him somehow, but that wouldn't be enough to make him release me.

"Fortunately, in my life, I don't live for moments." His fingers undid the button on my denim shorts.

I squeezed my eyes shut as I felt the fabric slide down my legs. Then, before finishing removing the shorts, my boots slipped off my feet with ease, and finally, he took off the denim shorts.

The senator positioned himself between my legs.

"Open your eyes, *sweetie*," he murmured, and when I did, his face was close to mine. "I've never seen a more beautiful creature..."

His lips touched mine, fitting perfectly, squeezing my waist, his tongue meeting mine in a slow, melodic dance. I let myself be carried away by the moment because, contrary to what Zachary had said, my life was made of moments.

Thinking it would be nearly impossible to get any more aroused, I realized that this man had the ability to drive me to ecstasy without even trying.

He slid his hand beneath my back, unclasping my bra.

"I wish I could tear off all these damn clothes," he grumbled, noticing my bra was also stuck to my arm.

"Your problems can be solved if you let me go." I missed the senator's soft lips when he pulled away.

"No, *sweetie*." He lifted my bra up, placing it with my elbow.

My nipples hardened from the ambient air, the man slowly guiding his eyes to my breasts. I gasped as Zachary's hands touched them, his fingers splayed there.

I'm not completely naive; I'm a curious woman. I knew how sex happened, had seen pornographic videos, and had touched myself with my own fingers. Like the women in those videos, I knew what pleasure was.

"Zachary." I gasped as his lips circled my nipple, his tongue passing over one while his hand squeezed the other.

He didn't stop, teasing me with his tongue as if playing with my other breast, squeezing it, then delightfully pinching my nipple. Alternating between the two, he left me breathless, with small moans escaping my lips.

It was a thousand times better than the videos I watched.

He paused mid-act, his lips descending down my belly, leaving small traces of kisses along the way, and holding the sides of my panties, he slowly removed them. I squeezed my eyes shut.

It was the first time a man saw me completely naked, and I couldn't even cover myself because my hands were bound.

"Don't be ashamed, beautiful Savannah, you're the most beautiful woman my eyes have ever seen," he whispered, noticing that my eyes were closed.

But I didn't open them, squeezing them even tighter as he spread my legs, bending them. I was completely exposed; nothing was left to prevent us from going through with it. At that moment, I would be forever marked by the senator.

His fingers touched my wet spot, delving further in, sliding through my folds.

"Savannah, open your eyes," his voice came out as an order, and I did.

The senator positioned himself over my legs, his face approaching my core, my eyes widening. His tongue touched my folds, a loud moan escaped my mouth; it felt like fire burning, a delicious flame driving me to delirium.

"*Zach... oh, Zach...*" I whined, pressing my pelvis harder against his face, which was between my legs.

I felt the glide all over my intimacy, taking me, claiming my virginity.

"Your pussy is as sweet as you are; it's impossible not to get addicted to this honey..." A little squeal escaped my mouth when he gave a small bite to the inside of my thigh, close to my pussy. "That's it, Savannah, don't hold back, scream, moan, give me everything..."

Zachary didn't stop, taking me to extreme peaks of pleasure, something I never thought possible. My body was on fire, droplets of sweat forming on my skin, all because a man was between my legs, taking me for himself.

When I thought he was going to let me come, the senator stopped.

"You'll come when my cock is inside you," he whispered, getting up on the bed. I could see traces of my pleasure on his beard.

The sexiest man I'd ever seen in my life.

Zachary began unbuttoning his shirt, taking it off to reveal his defined chest; he must have been into physical exercise. Then, the senator lowered his pants, his member outlined against his underwear. I should have closed my eyes, but my curiosity kept me from doing so. Without taking his eyes off me, he pulled down his underwear.

His cock brushed against his belly, big, extremely big, and it would penetrate me, taking my virginity.

"Senator," I whispered, starting to feel worried.

The man came over me, our eyes locked on each other.

"Do you use any contraceptive method?"

"No..." When I said that, he let out a long sigh.

"We'll need to use a condom, then. I'm not the type of man who goes around making babies." I just nodded, unable to say anything.

Zachary leaned over by the side of the bed, grabbed a gold envelope, opened it with his mouth, and put the condom on his member.

"Senator..." I called out, making him look at me. "I'd like to feel the texture of your member; I've never seen one before, and I don't know when it will happen again..."

I bit the corner of my lip, not even knowing where this boldness was coming from.

"Sweetie, I'm not letting you go; it won't be my cock you'll touch," he murmured reproachfully.

I realized that nothing I did would make him release me.

Zachary positioned himself between my legs, his cock entering me. I grimaced. The condom he was using felt like it was tearing me; the latex was very uncomfortable. I closed my eyes, waiting for him to take me completely, hoping the same pleasure would overwhelm me.

"Savannah, are you okay?" he asked. I opened my eyes.

"Yes, it's...," I lied.

"Your face says otherwise." He raised an eyebrow.

"It feels like you're tearing me apart, and the condom feels like it's burning..." I whined.

For long seconds, the senator stared at me.

"You know what, I'll do the withdrawal method." He pulled out, removing the condom.

"What does that mean?"

"I'll come outside," he said this time penetrating me without barriers.

"Is that safe?"

"I've done it before, and I've never gotten anyone pregnant." He shrugged, and I trusted him.

His cock took me as his, going deeper and deeper, penetrating me without barriers, tearing me apart, claiming me as his own. The senator's lips touched mine, starting a slow kiss.

The wet kiss was like disconnecting from the pain of losing my virginity, and when I realized it, the senator was already moving in and out, his cock thrusting with a little more force.

My moans were swallowed by his lips.

"*Oh... Zach*" I whimpered, intoxicated by pleasure.

Unable to contain myself, I started to grind against his thrusts; the pain was gone, completely replaced by pleasure. I wanted to touch him, feel him. I was motionless, as if the world had stopped, and it was just the two of us there.

"Fuck..." he rarely used profanity, and it made me even more excited.

The peak of my pleasure happened when I exploded, screaming in a loud moan. I bit his lip with some pressure, knowing that I had surrendered, writhing on the senator's cock.

"*Ah*, sweet Arizona girl... you're an addiction... I wish you were my addiction," he said, his lips pressed against mine.

Zachary groaned, gripping my hair at the back of my neck. I noticed he barely held on, and at the last moment, he pulled out.

"Fucking tight little pussy" was all he said as his body collapsed exhausted on top of mine.

CHAPTER SEVEN

Savannah

"Zach," I called his name as his body began to weigh heavily on mine. "I can't breathe."

The senator smiled as he got up, seeing his own cum on his belly, which had spread over our bodies when he fell on top of me.

"I'm going to get a cloth to clean you up," he said, turning and heading to the bathroom next door.

I didn't even have time to ask him to let me go; he left without giving me a chance to speak.

Zachary returned with a damp towel in his hand; he had cleaned himself up. He stopped by my side, rubbing the cloth over my belly, sliding it between my legs. Out of the corner of my eye, I saw him lift the towel, showing the stain of blood.

"I'm no longer a virgin," I whispered, catching the senator's attention, who seemed lost in thought.

"Savannah, we need to talk; there's something you need to know," he said with a serious expression.

"Could you at least let me out of this tie?" I asked with a half-smile.

"Yes, of course." Zachary leaned over, undoing the tie, and removed my shirt, which was tangled with my bra.

I propped myself up on my elbows, sitting on the bed. I directed my curious eyes toward that handsome man. Zach leaned over, pulling on his underwear, standing while putting it on.

I tried to do the same but couldn't find my panties anywhere. The senator sat back on the bed, extending his hand, and my fingers touched his.

"Is this the moment you're going to kick me out?" I joked with a smile.

"Could you stay here with me tonight?" he asked. I stopped beside him, straddling him and sitting facing the senator.

He had already seen me naked; there was nothing left to hide.

"I can't. I need to go; my aunt will worry," I whispered, raising my hand to try to touch his face, but his hand stopped me, holding my wrist.

"No touching, remember?" His voice had a slight reprimand.

"I thought it was only about sex." I deflated a little.

"Savannah, it's about everything. I don't want your touches..." The way he spoke made me realize he seemed to want me only for sex.

"Okay, I'd better go." I pulled my arm, trying to get off him, but the senator held me by the waist, making me lose my balance and fall back into his lap.

"I didn't say to leave." His voice always sounded as if he was commanding something.

"But I want to go. If I can't touch you, there's nothing I can do here. Just like you don't want me to touch you to avoid any connection, I don't want to be near you because I don't want to get attached to you," I declared quickly, turning my face to meet his intense blue eyes.

Zachary brought his face close to my hair, and I saw him take a deep breath as if he was inhaling my scent.

"You're right, it's selfish of me," he said, and at that moment, a noise was heard outside the room.

"Zach?" It was a man's voice.

"Fuck, it's my cousin," he whispered, getting up from the bed. "I'm coming, Willian."

He jumped out of bed, leaving me there, quickly pulling on his pants. He didn't even put on his shirt, turning to face me as he was almost at the door.

"Stay here, okay? Don't leave this room," he said again in a commanding tone.

I was left alone. The senator left the room. I grabbed my shorts; since I couldn't find my panties, I put them on without them. I quickly put on my bra and shirt, moving toward the door, doing what I did best: being curious. I pressed my face against the door and tried to listen to their conversation:

"Zachary, can you, for once in your life, think about us first and then about your cock?" The man sounded irritated.

"No one will find out; the girl is already leaving..."

"For God's sake, cousin! She's the girl you ran over. How did you manage to bring her to your apartment and have sex with her? Do you realize she could just be another scam artist?"

"She's not a scam artist!" I was relieved that at least Zachary had defended me.

"Based on what? On your cock that fucked the woman?" he retorted angrily.

The way they were talking made my heart beat so fast that I could swear the whole building could hear.

"William, I just know!" Zach roared.

"Fuck, this frustrates me so much. If only you could control yourself for once. Tomorrow is your damn wedding. Do you have any idea how negative this would be for our family if it appeared in a tabloid? Senator Zachary Fitzgerald dumps his beautiful fiancée for some girl from Arizona," he seemed to mock in his tone.

A buzzing filled my ears, my vision blurred, and all my mind kept repeating was: *he's getting married tomorrow.* Zachary is engaged?

I was a mistress?

I moved away from the door, automatically heading to the side of the bed where my phone had fallen to the floor. Even though the screen was cracked, it still worked.

I couldn't stay another minute in that place; I wasn't able to look at the face of the man who had just taken my virginity.

I put my phone in my pocket, no longer caring if his cousin was there. I went back to the door and opened it, expecting to see both men, but I only saw the senator alone.

"My cousin has left; we can continue our conversation," he said, turning his gaze back to me and only then realizing I was already dressed. "Savannah, what happened, and why are you crying?"

"No!" I stretched out my hand to keep Zachary from coming closer. "Did you think I was what? A whore? You made me a mistress!"

I sniffled loudly, feeling dirty, disgusted with myself for having enjoyed that first time.

"I can explain, Savannah, it's not what you think..."

"It's not? Aren't you getting married tomorrow?" I questioned, raising an eyebrow.

"Yes, I am, but..."

"Enough, Zachary. It's pointless to make excuses for something that has no explanation. You're engaged, you're getting married tomorrow; you just used me, and I knew that. So just let me go," I pleaded, almost begging.

"Let me give you my earbuds," he said, remembering our agreement.

"I don't want anything from you, I don't want anything that looks like you're paying for that sex..."

"Stop being ridiculous!" he cut me off but didn't stop me from walking.

I stopped in front of the door to his penthouse.

"Answer me one thing," I turned my neck to look at him. "Could I have ever been by your side?"

"No, Savannah, you're not the type of woman to be by a man like me." That was like a knife to my heart.

It hurt, it hurt like I had never felt before. He didn't even hesitate, answering bluntly, without any hesitation. I blinked several times, my eyes filled with tears.

"I hope I never see you again, senator. I hope you never know what it's like to be used and then abandoned at any moment. If it were up to me, I'd never want to see you again." I opened the door, hearing his footsteps behind me.

Before I could leave, Zachary's fingers grabbed my wrist.

"Let one of my drivers take you," he pleaded.

"I can manage perfectly fine on my own." I tried to pull my arm away, giving him one last look into those blue eyes.

"Our agreement is still valid; you'll always be my first virgin girl..."

"That doesn't matter anymore, not after knowing you're a liar." Zachary didn't want to let go of my wrist.

"I didn't lie, I just omitted something..."

"You omitted something essential. I wasn't born to be a mistress; you hurt me, made me think I could be the one, but none of it was real. As you said, I'm not the woman to be by your side..."

"You're misunderstanding, Savannah," he muttered, sounding irritated.

"We won't see each other again. We don't need to explain anything. I'd rather leave here with the feeling of abandonment than think I have any hope. If you can't commit to anyone, not even to your fiancée, don't do it. Don't break hearts..."

I pulled my arm with more force at that moment, and he released it, freeing me from his touch. I quickly moved to the elevator door, which opened—at least that was on my side.

Zach even tried to follow me, but I pressed the button for the doors to close quickly. I didn't want to see that face anymore, didn't want to feel the despair, knowing that tomorrow would be his wedding, and I was the mistress.

I didn't stop the tears from falling, wanting only to be alone at that moment.

I lowered my face, realizing I was barefoot. *Shit*! I forgot my boots. How did I not notice I was without them?

CHAPTER EIGHT

Zachary

"Don't leave the girl alone, even if you have to drag her, I don't want her walking barefoot," I ordered my security.

I ran my hand through my hair as if I could pull out the strands in frustration. My bare feet pacing around my penthouse, it wasn't supposed to end this way, Savannah wasn't supposed to leave here dazed.

I wanted to explain things to her; it was clear the girl knew nothing about me, not even that I had a fiancée.

Her tears still echoed in my mind. I was a complete jerk; I had no right to take her virginity and then snub her. Women like Savannah were like Lucy; they touched the hearts of every man, ensnaring them and keeping them in their grasp with their sweetness.

Nothing I try to justify in my mind can excuse what I did to that small woman. It had been a long time since I'd seen such a rarity in front of me; I was enchanted, I let myself be carried away by my body's desires, wanting to feel the texture of having one more of those in my hands. Then it was just a matter of sending her away. It would be easy, just like it was easy for Lucy to abandon me.

But Savannah had something Lucy didn't have—the way she looked at me, claiming me as hers. I almost let go of her hands several times, but I knew that doing so would be my ultimate downfall.

Deep down, it was better that it ended the way it did, so we wouldn't risk ending up face to face again.

I entered my room, her boot still there, proof that the girl from Arizona was real. How could I have thought this would be just another ordinary day? Nothing about it was normal, starting with that little sweet treat who threw herself in front of my car.

On the nightstand next to the bed, I saw my phone vibrating, the word "Dad" flashing. I let out a long sigh, knowing he was already aware of what had happened. Ignoring his call would be worse, so I approached, picked up the phone, and answered. Before he could start talking, I could hear Dad huffing.

"Go on, unload," I murmured, sitting on my bed.

"*Zachary Fitzgerald, do you have any idea how many sensationalist websites we had to pay to keep the girl's face out of the spotlight?*" Dad began grumbling.

"Thanks, I don't want her face associated with any site," I declared, my eyes fixed on her boot on the floor.

"*William said she was here.*"

"She was, but not anymore, thanks to Will. Savannah left here thinking I was a complete bastard, not that I'm not, but she shouldn't have left like that." My sigh clearly put Dad on alert.

"*Did you like her?*" No one understood me better than Arnold.

"Savannah is different, which makes her impossible for me." I turned my face, still seeing the rumpled sheets where her long blonde hair had been spread out.

"*You know not all women are like Lucy.*" Lucy would always be a ghost in my life.

"Yes, Dad, Savannah might not be like her, but she was sweet, smiling, acting like she didn't know who I was, even arguing with me. Damn, that girl is clueless; maybe I should put a bodyguard on her?" I spoke rapidly.

"*Let's take it step by step. You've come to all these conclusions in just one morning; how do we know she wasn't lying about you?*"

"Simple, from her look. She wanted to take a photo with me just to brag to her dad, who apparently likes politics, unlike her."

"Alright, as for the bodyguard part, no, you're not going to do that. We can't have any connection with the woman. Tomorrow is your wedding, but there's still time to back out." Everyone in my family knew my marriage to Hanna would never be real.

They saw her as a family member; in Mom's mind, she might even develop some feelings, but that was practically impossible.

"No, I can't let my friend down; I promised her that," I said firmly.

"We're talking about a lifetime together; I married your mother for love, and I wanted the same for my son." The way my parents loved each other was something to envy.

Or rather, envy me. My mother was a woman completely disconnected from politics; she was Lucy in my father's life, but their love was stronger, and she managed to stay by his side. Unlike my mother, who felt overwhelmed, chose to run away, and I let her.

"Hanna is a comfortable choice, Dad. I don't want to risk bumping into women who aren't right for me anymore."

"Then everything will be easier if you stop running over women and bringing them to your penthouse." Dad had that mocking tone.

"That's something I just added to my list of things not to do anymore."

"Everyone in the family will thank you for not having to remove your name from the websites." I could swear he was rolling his eyes at that moment.

"I promise that after what I did today, I won't make the same mistake again," I murmured, still feeling like a bastard for what I did to Savannah.

"What exactly are we talking about?"

"Dad, Savannah didn't know I was engaged; she was a virgin. I took her virginity. I was a real bastard." Arnold let out a sigh of reprimand.

"*Zachary, that's not how I raised you. Definitely don't do that again. We'll keep an eye on her in the coming weeks to make sure she stays quiet. We don't want our family's name linked to any gossip site that loves exposing us.*" He was right.

"If you want, I'll even accept one of your punishments," I murmured, my mockery lacking humor.

"*Your punishment will be facing your mother because I'll tell her everything, from start to finish. We both know her sermons are better than mine...*"

"Dad..."

He ended the call. And I was left there with the boots of my Arizona girl. What did I do?

What did I cause in Savannah's life? Could I, for once in my life, think about someone other than myself?

At that moment, all I wanted was to run after her and beg for her forgiveness, to tell her I wanted her by my side. Is there such a thing as love at first sight? Because if it exists, I might have fallen for that Arizona woman, but tomorrow I have a wedding to attend—my wedding.

CHAPTER NINE

Savannah

"Miss?" Through the car's rearview mirror, I saw the driver calling me. He was a young man, wearing a suit with a small symbol of the family he worked for, the Fitzgeralds. "Are you feeling better?"

"Yes..."

That was all I said. After all, I was practically forced into that car. According to the security guard at the scene, the senator insisted that I get into the car. All I wanted was for the senator to go to hell.

How could I have been so foolish? Why didn't I research Zachary beforehand? Maybe I would have discovered that he was getting married and wouldn't have been his mistress. I felt guilty, humiliated by the woman he betrayed.

"I don't know what happened, but the senator is a good man." I squinted at the driver.

"Really? I don't want to talk about your senator," I grumbled, staring at the road.

My tears had dried, leaving only anger and hatred. I had held myself back for years, only to give myself to a committed man? All for a moment? For thinking that he might be my Prince Charming, making my first time special.

What a fool I was!

"Sorry, miss, I didn't mean to upset you further." Our eyes met again through the rearview mirror. "Are you new to the city? I wasn't the one driving the senator's car when the incident happened, I hope you weren't seriously injured."

"I'm fine, as good as it gets," I said irritably, realizing the driver was just trying to be kind.

The driver didn't try to engage in further conversation and followed his GPS route. I wasn't usually this selfish and enraged; I was always pleasant to those around me. I felt bad for being rude to the driver, so I started to talk:

"My name is Savannah. I arrived here in Sacramento last night from Arizona." I saw the man smile.

"Nice to meet you, Savannah. I noticed you didn't have the best first day in our city. By the way, my name is Michael. I don't work for the senator; I'm a driver for his father. But since one of the senator's drivers fell ill, I was reassigned to him."

"Lucky you, then," I said, smiling, making him furrow his brow.

"Indeed, I don't know what the senator did that was so severe, but I hope he can be forgiven." He signaled, and I recognized my aunt's street.

"What he did is unforgivable. I don't want to see that senator, not even painted in gold," I rolled my eyes.

The car slowed down and stopped in front of my aunt's house. Michael looked over his shoulder, not turning off the car.

"Thank you for the chat, Michael." I gave a brief smile.

"You're a lovely girl, Savannah. Don't let it get you down, no matter what happened with the senator. If you want, you could give me your number. I could take you out for a tour around Sacramento sometime. Us Californians owe you that for your disastrous first day." It was hard not to like Michael.

"Just as friends, right?" I said, twisting my lip into a grimace.

"Of course."

I gave him my number and said goodbye. He even got out of the car to open the door for me. With a brief wave, he drove away.

Michael was a handsome man, not drop-dead gorgeous, but good-looking. With brown hair, a smooth face, and an average height. Maybe if he had been the one to hit me, I wouldn't have ended up in his bed. He seemed like someone who would take me to a pub for coffee until he was sure I was okay, unlike the senator, who took his concern further, even inviting me to his penthouse.

But as the old saying goes, if one doesn't want it, two can't have it.

I wanted it; I didn't regret how I lost my virginity. I was sure I would never forget him. But what followed made me detest my first time.

I hadn't even reached the front door of the house when I saw it being opened abruptly by my aunt. Her eyes were worried, even tearful.

"Sav, where have you been? Your phone has been off; I was worried." My aunt pulled me into her arms, relieved that I was there with her.

I accepted her embrace, which was meant to be comforting but triggered a new flood of tears.

"Auntie." I sniffled, unable to contain my loud sniffle.

"Oh, dear, what happened?" She held my hand as we went to the living room.

I sat on a sofa, covering my face with my hand, hiding my eyes, feeling ashamed of what I had done. Where was the woman who had felt brave enough to make a difference?

Auntie patted my hands and made me remove them from my face, being attentive, showing how much she cared.

"I... I..." I mumbled, "I'll understand if you don't want me here anymore."

"My dear, what could be so serious?"

With great effort, I began to recount everything, from the moment of the accident to ending up in the senator's bed. I could feel my face flush when I admitted that I was no longer a virgin. At no point did Aunt Brianna judge me; she always encouraged me to talk more.

After I finished confessing everything, there was a deafening silence in the house. Then, finally, she spoke:

"Well, I don't think your father needs to know about this," Brianna tried to smile.

"You're not going to send me away?" I lowered my face, feeling embarrassed.

"Sweetie, I always thought it was absurd that you were 22 and still a virgin. Your father raised you and your sister in a glass bubble, where everything seems perfect. Savannah, this is the real world; men will always think with their lower head first. That's why I never want one in my life. We'll get through this. Soon you'll be in another man's warm bed, and it will definitely be someone worth it, not someone who makes you cry right after." Auntie wiped my tears with her hands, always having a lighter view of life and not taking things too seriously. "Let's face it, that family of politicians is attractive, but we'll get over them."

She winked conspiratorially. Talking everything out with Auntie felt good, like a weight was lifted off my shoulders. She understood me.

"I think my body is tired from all the crying," I declared, deflated.

"Go take a shower, Sav. I'll prepare something to eat, and another time we'll go out to explore the city properly." We stood up from the sofa together.

I headed towards my room. Auntie had even made a room for me in her house. My bare feet reminded me that I would never see my boots again. I was too proud to confront the senator just to ask for them back.

He threw in my face that I wasn't worthy of being with him, and that was reason enough to hate him.

CHAPTER TEN

Savannah

Two years and eight months later...

The TV was announcing Christopher Fitzgerald's candidacy, his cousin... With a frustrated sigh, I grabbed the remote and turned off the screen.

There had been an initial vote for the public to choose between the two parties who would run for president. This was Christopher's first run for the presidency of America. If he won, he would be the youngest president to ever sit in that chair.

The pride of the powerful Fitzgerald clan, and what was my surprise to learn that Zachary Fitzgerald would be alongside his cousin as vice president. From what Auntie had explained to me, if Christopher won, Zachary would also become the president of the Senate.

Great, that Greek god was now gracing the screens of all Americans, just like his cousin, the perfect pair.

"Mommy..." My eyes fell on the little one building with colorful blocks in the center of the living room floor.

Sadie was losing patience with a block that wouldn't fit, banging one piece against another.

"Sweetie, let Mommy show you how to do it." I sat down on the floor next to my daughter.

Sadie raised her chubby little hands towards me, handing over the two blocks.

"See, everything has a way." I demonstrated how to fit the blocks together.

She didn't even glance away with her blue eyes, focused intently on the task, always very attentive.

Sadie was one year and eleven months old, soon to be two, the time I had set for myself to wait before revealing her existence to her father. I just didn't expect him to be a possible candidate alongside his cousin.

Zachary was one of America's most eligible bachelors. The fact that he had been left standing at the altar made him a pitiful figure. This made all those women think they could desire him in their beds, to take care of him, not knowing that this man was a complete scoundrel.

The pinnacle was reading that the California senator had been left at the altar; the bride hadn't shown up and ran off with another man, whom she married and was expecting a child with. This made Zachary the most beloved cuckold.

I felt so much pity for him it almost made me sick. Zachary was nothing like the magazines portrayed; he was a scoundrel, a top-notch villain. He made that clear at the many events he attended with various women.

Where did the old image of candidates needing a family go? In the new generation of Fitzgeralds, none of them were married, or at least not up to the present moment. Christopher was a widower, and according to what I read in the magazines, he was the most beloved widower, completely obsessed with his work. The current governor of California, William Fitzgerald, another cousin, had a fiancée. But who could guarantee that they weren't all cut from the same cloth?

I focused on my little one, how she had many traits of the Fitzgeralds, but deep down she was all mine, just mine, and no one would ever take her from me. If there was anything good that Zachary had brought, it was this little girl.

I couldn't lie; when those two lines appeared on the pharmacy test, I felt my whole world collapse beneath me. I was pregnant and scared. How would I tell Auntie, my father? I thought that would be the moment Auntie would send me away. But to my surprise, she was radiant.

With her help, I told Daddy. Of course, he nearly had a heart attack and wanted to come to Sacramento to kill the man who touched me. For that reason, I never revealed who Sadie's father was. When asked, I said it was a man I met and lost contact with afterward. It seemed too superficial and empty, but I couldn't go around saying that my daughter's father was the senator. That might make him come after her and cause a huge commotion.

"How is the prettiest little girl in the country?" Hazel appeared, rubbing her eyes, revealing that she had just woken up.

"Taking the chance to sleep, sis?" I teased, looking up at my sister.

"Tomorrow starts my classes," she grumbled, heading to the kitchen.

"Did everything go smoothly with your transfer?" I asked.

"Yes, it did," she said a bit louder from the kitchen.

I got up from the floor and motioned for my little one to come with me. Sadie held onto my fingers as we walked towards my sister.

"Are you going to put Michael's plan into action?" Hazel asked while preparing her coffee.

"I don't know; it would be too cowardly to get close to his family." I lifted my little one and seated her in the high chair.

"Think of the positives, sis. You'll have a salary, you'll be able to prepare to tell the senator everything, study the territory, meet his mother, and have Michael around. Sadie could stay with a caretaker only in the mornings; the Blossom's daughter is a good girl, she studies in the afternoon, takes care of Sadie in the mornings, and I'll take over when I get back from college. This is your chance, Sav."

Michael was the first friend I made in California, and after he gave me that ride, we never stopped talking. I would never hide my pregnancy from him, but he respected my timing. He worked as a driver for the Fitzgeralds, Zachary's parents.

Finally, a cleaning position opened up at their house. Michael, being friends with the housekeeper, recommended me. She asked me to come to the house this afternoon, when Mrs. Grace would be home. It seemed she liked to meet each employee personally.

The interview had been scheduled for a week, and the big moment had arrived: to go or not to go. To be near my daughter's father, risking revealing my secret and possibly being abandoned once again.

CHAPTER ELEVEN

Savannah

I parked my truck in the back of the Fitzgerald residence, as Michael had instructed. Only the homeowners used the main entrance.

According to my friend, the senator was in Washington D.C. with his cousin, making some adjustments for their campaign, and he was barely showing up at his parents' house.

Being here didn't mean my spot was guaranteed; I still had the interview with Grace Fitzgerald and Mary Cabot, the housekeeper.

I got out of my truck, running my fingers through my straight hair, checking the rearview mirror to make sure I looked okay. Luckily, the last time I had the truck serviced, it hadn't broken down again. I was sharing it with my sister. Hazel came to California to help me take care of Sadie. After all, I wanted to work; I couldn't live off my father forever.

And that was just an excuse for my sister to come rushing to my side. We had always been very close; she wanted to come earlier, but Daddy always found an excuse to keep her there.

My father still saw us as his little girls. With Mom's help, we always got what we wanted. But obviously, Mr. Peter Bellingham only allowed my sister to leave Arizona when she was on birth control, as he didn't want lightning to strike twice in the same place.

My father loved Sadie and always complained about her living so far from him. If it weren't for the farm we had in Arizona, I was sure he would have already moved to California.

I turned my face when I heard footsteps approaching, and I opened a brief smile when I saw Michael. He was wearing the Fitzgerald uniform, with a small emblem on the corner of his jacket.

"I thought I'd have to send Hazel to drag you here," he said with a big smile, reaching into his pants pocket.

I approached him, and we exchanged a quick kiss on the cheek. Michael was only about two centimeters taller than me. At the start of our friendship, we had even shared a kiss after a date, but it didn't progress. I soon discovered I was pregnant, and my thoughts were entirely on my daughter.

Michael was understanding and said he would wait for me. Although I feared that waiting might eventually come, I knew he would never be like the senator. Michael was the right man for any woman: a friend, caring, and he liked Sadie, treating her like a niece.

"I'm nervous, and I don't even know why." A forced smile appeared on my lips.

"It's a job interview; who stays calm for a job interview?" Michael patted my back, helping me toward the entrance.

We always walked like this, close to each other. From the outside, it might have seemed like we were a couple, but I saw him as a brother. I didn't want to ruin what we had built. I was afraid that if we started dating, and eventually broke up, our friendship would end with it.

We climbed the two flights of stairs. Michael opened the door leading to the kitchen. There was a lady standing by the counter, holding a notebook.

"Mary, this is Savannah, the friend I told you about," Michael said, drawing the lady's attention to us.

She immediately started evaluating my appearance, as if judging whether I was suited for the job.

The woman stepped away from the counter, closed her notebook, walked towards me, and extended her hand in a gesture of greeting.

"It's a pleasure, Mrs. Savannah Bellingham." She knew all my details. "I'm the housekeeper for the Fitzgeralds."

"Thank you for the opportunity," I said with a brief smile.

"Come with me, Mrs. Grace is waiting for us in her office." I merely nodded, as the lady did not offer a smile.

I said goodbye to Michael and followed the housekeeper. We passed through the enormous kitchen, where meals were clearly prepared. There wasn't even a table for the family. My curiosity was piqued when an open door revealed a vast dining room.

"As you can see, the house is a bit large." "A bit?" I almost asked if she was being modest. "We have a team of five cleaners, each responsible for a different area of the house, but at the moment, we are short one, so you won't be responsible for the entire house."

I couldn't help but sigh in relief. We passed a staircase with golden railings and white steps; everything was very white and incredibly beautiful, like a scene from a soap opera.

Stopping in front of a door, the housekeeper knocked twice, entered the room, and held the doorknob for me to go in first. My curious eyes were always scanning everything around me. Wow, the office was beautiful. Why was I still surprised? My daughter was a part of all this, and it terrified me just to think about it. I didn't know how far this absurd amount of money was a good thing.

"Mrs. Grace, this is the candidate for the interview, Savannah Bellingham." The woman sitting in a large chair behind the desk stood up and extended her hand to me.

I walked up to her, taking her elegant hand. I knew she was the senator's mother, having seen her in the newspapers, always impeccably styled, whether her hair was loose or done up.

"Welcome, Savannah," she called me by my first name.

"Oh... it's a pleasure." I offered a half-smile.

Mrs. Grace didn't take her eyes off me, as if she already knew me, which was impossible. There was no way she could know who I was—the insignificant case of her son.

"Please, have a seat, dear." She pointed to a chair, and I took it. "I was reading your file; do you have a daughter?"

"Yes, I do," I nodded as I spoke.

"Have you never worked before?" My file didn't list any previous jobs.

"No, Sadie is about to turn two, and with my sister's help, I can finally get a job. I didn't want to leave my little one with someone I didn't trust." I was honest.

Mrs. Grace asked several questions, including whether my daughter had an involved father, and I said no. Even the housekeeper beside me seemed surprised by the amount of information being asked.

After several minutes, Grace placed a few papers on the desk and smiled broadly.

"Welcome to our home. You can start tomorrow; we need someone as soon as possible." Turning to Mary, she said, "Give Savannah a uniform, and I expect to see her tomorrow."

Lastly, she looked at me. At that moment, I didn't know whether to smile, cry, or laugh nervously. I was closer than I had thought to seeing Senator Zachary Fitzgerald again after almost three years.

CHAPTER TWELVE

Savannah

My first day at the Fitzgerald house was calm. I was assigned to clean the first floor, accompanied by Olivia, a very chatty girl, which was actually wonderful since it made the hours fly by.

"This job becomes a real treat when the senator and his cousins are around," Olivia whispered beside me as we cleaned the doors and windows at the back of the house.

"Oh, heavens," I murmured back with a smile.

I didn't want to fuel that conversation. All I wanted was to avoid talking about the senator.

"You know, those men are completely untouchable for mere mortals like us. I'm very realistic; if only Michael would look at me." She sighed dreamily.

"Do you like Mitch?" I asked with a mischievous smile.

"Wow, what familiarity is this? The last thing I need is to be here praising the man who is your boyfriend." She widened her eyes at me.

"No, no." I shook my head vigorously. "We're just friends."

"Lucky you." She smiled.

"Michael is the easiest person to talk to I've ever met. Haven't you ever spoken to him?" I frowned, confused.

"Savannah, every time I'm in front of him, I freeze. He probably thinks I'm missing a few screws." I couldn't help but smile at that.

We continued working without much conversation, as Mary started keeping an eye on us, clearly observing my work.

Working at the Fitzgerald residence was nice, or at least that's how my first day made it seem. We finished the windows, put our supplies in our cart, and went through the back to avoid bumping into the lady of the house.

The rest of the day was quiet, with no incidents, and by the end, I even received a compliment from Mary for being quiet and not making a fuss about working in a house of famous politicians. We weren't even allowed to use our phones, so if my sister needed me, she would have to call Mary—the only number available.

"HOW IS THE JOB GOING?" my aunt asked at breakfast.

"In three days of work, I've only seen his face in photographs. Mrs. Grace is a quiet woman; I hardly ever see her, she's almost never home. She's exactly as she appears on TV—elegant and discreet." This wasn't a lie; the way Mrs. Grace moved around the house was always with poise, and when she spoke, it was calm and soft.

"You know he could show up there at any moment," my sister spoke up.

Hazel was eating quickly to drop me off at college and then head to work.

"Yes, I know, but I could bet he won't even remember me. I'm pretty sure the senator has had countless women in his bed; I was just one more," I grumbled, shrugging my shoulders slightly.

"Look, from my point of view, you're not just one more woman. The senator hasn't forgotten you. If he had, he would have started a relationship with someone else," Hazel was trying to be confident.

"Sister, we're talking about a man who's infamous for being left at the altar, who every woman wants to warm his bed, and besides, he can date whoever he wants without losing his fame. Everyone firmly believes he's the passionate man who was deceived." I rolled my eyes.

Hazel, Aunt Brianna, and Michael were the only ones who knew about Sadie's paternity.

My little one patted the high chair.

"Maix, maix, maix..." I smiled at that little one who had my heart in the palm of her hand; I loved that little girl unconditionally.

"She loves the tapioca cookies you make for her," my aunt said with affection.

"We'll need to restock soon." I nodded, placing two new cookies on her high chair. "The hardest part is leaving her at home."

My voice softened as I lost myself looking at Sadie, my little one with an easy smile, blonde hair, and blue eyes—my little doll.

"Tell your mommy that Auntie loves spending the mornings with you."

In the end, my aunt changed her work hours, staying home in the mornings so that Sadie could spend her mornings with Aunt Brianna and afternoons with my sister. At night, I stayed close to my little one.

I PARKED MY TRUCK IN the staff area, slung my bag over my shoulder. Inside it was my uniform, which I would change into in the staff bathroom. Michael's car wasn't there; he must have been at work.

I entered the house through the back door and went straight to change to start my day. I ran into Mary as I was leaving the bathroom, leaving my bag in the locker inside. The bathroom also served as the locker room; it was a large room with shower stalls and sinks.

"Good morning, Mary," I greeted her by her first name, as she had asked us to.

"Good morning, Savannah." She nodded with a brief smile. "Mr. Arnold arrived from his trip this morning, so you might run into him. I kindly ask that you avoid any encounter if possible, and if it does happen, don't be a starstruck fan."

"Oh, I definitely won't do that," I joked, shaking my head.

"We've had staff members who did that, and it's embarrassing. Mr. Fitzgerald, although a good man, doesn't appreciate that kind of approach." Mary wrinkled her lips, clearly recalling such incidents.

Mary was a good housekeeper and always made us feel comfortable around her.

Olivia would arrive an hour after me, so I started working without her. I said goodbye to Mary and headed to the cleaning area, grabbed my cart, and went to the library, which was my task for the day.

The house was as quiet as ever; I could almost swear the Fitzgeralds were still asleep. At that hour, it was permissible to pass through the living room with the cleaning cart since no one was supposed to be there, or at least that's what the house's schedule regulation stated.

Distracted, I passed through the room, startled when I looked up and saw the former president sitting on the sofa with his wife beside him.

"Oh, I'm so sorry, I didn't know..." My sentence trailed off as they both looked at me. I felt my face heat up from embarrassment and fear that I might have misread the regulations that day.

"It's alright, dear, we just decided to sit here before having our breakfast," Grace said, her voice as calm as ever, with a small smile.

It almost seemed like they had done it on purpose, as if they knew I would pass by.

"Oh, I'm so sorry, I'm here wondering if I might have misread the regulations..."

"No, you didn't misread," Grace was the only one speaking to me. "By the way, you haven't met my husband. This is Arnold Fitzgerald."

The man stood up from the sofa; he was tall, like his son, with gray hair and light brown eyes, unlike Zachary, who must have inherited his mother's darker eye color.

I wondered if they introduced Mr. Arnold to all new staff members. That question lingered in my mind.

"Savannah Bellingham, is that right?" His voice was just as I had imagined, the same as on TV.

"Yes, sir, it's a pleasure. Could we take a picture together to show my father?" I quickly composed myself, realizing I had made an inappropriate joke. Damn my tendency to joke at inopportune moments. Mr. Fitzgerald narrowed his eyes at me. "Shit, I've said too much, it's a terrible habit when I'm nervous. Shit, I said shit... if you'll excuse me, I'm just making things worse..."

The former president smiled right at me, and his wife joined him.

"I love how you're so unfiltered. Few people are like that in our circle," Grace said, placing her hand on her husband's arm.

"It must be very boring, at most tedious." I smiled back, still feeling my face warm.

"You can't imagine how much," Mr. Fitzgerald replied.

Together, they were the opposite of what I had expected—friendly and accommodating.

"If you'll excuse me, if Mary catches me chatting, I'll get a brief scolding." I grabbed my cart again.

"I hope to bump into you again, Miss Bellingham." Arnold made me smile warmly at him.

"Well, I can tell my father that you're taller than him, which was a topic at one of our dinners," I added, obviously talking too much.

"I can imagine how lively your dinners must be," Grace shook her head.

"A Bellingham member in this house would make the walls vibrate with how much we love to laugh and speak out of turn."

I could easily have kept chatting with them, but they were too busy, and I had my work to do, so I followed my route.

CHAPTER THIRTEEN

Savannah

After a week working at the Fitzgeralds' house, I could say with all honesty that Mrs. Grace was a charming woman. Whenever I crossed paths with her in a corridor, she would take some time to chat, which, according to Olivia, was quite strange since Mrs. Grace wasn't known for engaging much with the staff.

Maybe if I gained her trust, it might be easier to mention that my daughter was her granddaughter.

Mr. Arnold spent most of his time in his office when he was at home or went to the California State Capitol, where the government headquarters was located. I didn't know his position there, but according to Grace, Arnold was retired but couldn't disconnect from work.

"Savannah, dear?" I heard Mrs. Fitzgerald's voice call out as I was passing through the back of the house.

I turned my face, noticing a beautiful young woman with long hair standing next to her. Both of them smiled at me, and I saw the girl give Mrs. Fitzgerald a brief nudge.

"Yes, Mrs. Grace." I just smiled, wondering who this girl was. Could Zachary really be involved with someone so young?

"I wanted to introduce you to my daughter, Scarlett." I almost let out a sigh of relief, but I managed to restrain myself.

"Oh, it's a pleasure." I brushed my hand over my uniform, even though I knew it was clean, accepting the girl's handshake.

Scarlett shook my hand firmly and even gave me a quick hug, not caring that I was just the cleaner. She was a tall woman, and unlike Zachary, seemed much younger.

"Mom talks a lot about you. You're even more beautiful than she said." She flashed a lovely smile as she pulled away.

"Oh, I'm speechless." I felt my face start to heat up from embarrassment.

"My birthday is tomorrow, so I'll be around. I hope we can talk another time." I just nodded, controlling myself to avoid making any inappropriate jokes.

The two of them moved away, and as I turned, I saw Olivia coming toward me. She had witnessed the interaction between mother and daughter.

"When I say the treatment is different, this is what I mean, Sav. No other staff member has been introduced to their daughter. Scarlett comes here rarely because she started college this year, and I confess I've never seen her being introduced before. Friend, there's something more to this." Olivia helped me move the carts to the cleaning area.

"What could be different about me? I'm here like any other employee, working just like everyone else," I said as we walked down the corridor.

"That's a mystery." We entered the cleaning room.

As we pondered, we put away all the products we wouldn't need anymore. There was only an hour left of work.

"Could it be that you're some lost daughter of theirs, and now they're studying your life?" Olivia threw out a theory, making me turn my face toward her and see her eyes sparkle with her far-fetched idea.

"Olivia, obviously not. I look just like my mother and have the same birthmark as my father. Your theory has no basis." I shook my head, struggling not to laugh.

Of course, there was a reason they were getting close to me, but that possibility wasn't on the table. How would they know I had a fling with

Zachary? It was so brief that they obviously didn't even have time to remember my name.

"Damn, that was the only thing that came to mind," Olivia crossed her arms, thoughtful. "There's no reason for them to treat you differently."

"Can we change the subject?" I asked as something occurred to me. "It's Friday, what do you think about coming to my place? I'll invite Michael..."

I smiled with a hint of mischief. Olivia was a lively woman, just the kind Mitch liked, and I wanted to see my friend happy. "Why not give it a try?"

"Seriously? Like, really serious?" Olivia made a face, looking for some hint of joking from me.

"Do I look like someone who jokes around? Of course, I'm serious." I shook my head, grabbing the brooms since we needed to clean the small tea room. It wasn't big, so it would be quick.

"Savannah, have I told you that I love you today?" she teased, and we both headed to our last cleaning spot.

Some staff worked on Saturdays and Sundays, but since our work was only on the ground floor and the tasks could easily be organized during the week, our work hours were shorter.

I spent the entire cleaning of the tea room listening to Olivia talk about her dresses and asking for help deciding which one to wear. I gave my tips based on what I thought looked nice, though I didn't care much for that sort of thing.

I wanted to set them up, but I had forgotten to invite Michael for the dinner. I knew he would accept; Mitch always did.

With Olivia's help, we finished cleaning with the last sofa done. I let out a long sigh, turning my gaze to my coworker.

"Do we need to go all the way around, or can we pass through the room?" I asked, amidst my exhaustion from the day's work.

"I checked the schedule, and it's allowed at this time, but with Miss Scarlett being here, and when the daughter is in the house, their whole routine gets messed up," Olivia concluded.

"Just to be safe, I think it's better to go around the back, don't you think?" I made a face, and Olivia did too.

"Yeah..." We both shrugged. Going through the room would get us to the cleaning area faster, but going around meant leaving the house and walking around it.

"Well, it's just a *short walk*, let's go." I started gathering our cleaning supplies, placing them in the cart.

Olivia took charge of pushing the cart while I walked beside her and closed the door behind me. As we walked down the corridor in silence, I heard footsteps coming from the opposite direction. My head snapped up abruptly when I caught the scent of that perfume, which was like a blast from the past.

Our eyes met, and I felt my face flush, as if the entire world had stopped around me, a buzzing taking over my ear. There he was, the same man who had taken my virginity and made a point to say I wasn't his type, only to abandon me without a care, not even bothering to follow up when I was left at the altar. Everything he said that day, when we were together, was a lie, *a lie*!

"Savannah, what are you doing here?" The way he said my first name burst the bubble, the buzzing dissipated, and I returned to reality.

"This is my job, if you'll excuse me." I didn't smile at him, but I did smile at his father, who was standing beside him. "Mr. Arnold."

"Miss Bellingham." The former president smiled back at me as I passed by them.

"What the fuck is this, Dad?" I could hear Zachary's growl of anger.

He was still the same, the impeccable, handsome, and wonderful Senator Fitzgerald, and that's why I was here—to find a way to tell my daughter's father that we had a baby. A beautiful baby girl.

CHAPTER FOURTEEN

Zachary

"Can someone explain to me what Savannah Bellingham is doing here?" I ran my hand through my hair in frustration as I entered the room, seeing my father, mother, and sister all present.

"Do you know her, little brother?" Scarlett had that pout on her lips she always made when she wanted to show she didn't know something.

"Don't give me that crap, because I won't believe it. Everyone here knows who that girl is. What the hell is she doing in my family's house?" I was angry, furious about whatever they were scheming behind my back.

"Nothing, Zachary. There's nothing being schemed here. One of our drivers recommended her to Mary; I think he's her boyfriend. The girl is a great worker, does her job well. I didn't see a problem since you're about to move to Washington D.C. to be with Chris. Besides, she never mentioned your name even once; I believe she's already forgotten you just as you have forgotten her," Mom said, shrugging her shoulders, looking for a reaction from me.

Forgotten? That was what I wanted everyone to believe, that I had forgotten that little cowgirl with loose hair, slightly tanned skin, intense blue eyes. Damn! It was as if everything inside me had reignited, turning a small ember into a huge flame.

"How do they know she has a boyfriend?" I asked, knowing I would regret that question.

"I see them together in their free time," Mom shrugged as if it was no big deal.

Had I been so insignificant to her? Had Savannah moved on? What did I expect? That she would wait for me until her death? I shouldn't, but I was slightly unsettled by that realization, another man touching that sweet girl.

Not thinking about her was easier, so those jealous thoughts wouldn't come, but now they were there. Knowing Savannah was near and yet distant was going to eat me alive.

"They shouldn't have hired her. They shouldn't have brought that girl into this house," I roared, clenching my fists in anger and jealousy. At that moment, Savannah appeared, making it clear she had heard what I said.

She wasn't wearing her uniform anymore but rather tight jeans, a white tank top, and a damn pair of boots, just like the ones that had tormented me in my apartment, never letting me forget the sweet girl from Arizona.

"I... I'm sorry," she stammered, her cheeks reddening with her obvious awkwardness. She was still the same girl I had known.

"Dear, is there a problem?" My mother stood up from the couch.

"N... no, I was just finishing cleaning the cart. I found this little bracelet and thought it might belong to one of you." On her small, delicate fingers was a small piece of jewelry I recognized as belonging to Scarlett, as she was the one who wore such jewelry.

"It's mine. I was searching through my bags for it. Thank you, Savannah." My sister went to the woman, who handed her the bracelet.

What the hell, they even addressed her by her first name.

I couldn't move, couldn't take my eyes off Savannah, the way her body moved, her full lips slightly pursed with fear. Her hair tied back in a ponytail made it clear it was still long.

"Mrs. Grace, I apologize, and I understand if you want to fire me," Savannah's words made me feel like the worst kind of monster, the cruelest there was. How could I do this to her?

"You don't need to apologize. The job is yours, unless you don't want it," Mom said, and Savannah turned her face, our eyes meeting.

"They know who you are, rest assured. They did this to set up a meeting between us. If it were another time, I might believe it, but not now." I directed an irritated look at my father and mother.

They had no right to put Savannah in that situation.

"They know who I am?" Savannah turned her face toward my mother, not understanding what I meant.

"Yes, dear, we know who you are. We were surprised when you were recommended to work here. At first, yes, we thought we might bring you two together, but we know you have a boyfriend since we've seen you with the driver numerous times, and we've grown quite fond of your presence. So, we kept you here for who you are, not because of my son."

"N... boyfriend?" Savannah cleared her throat and I could swear that my mother, who was turned away from me, made some gesture to her. "Oh, yes, Mitch is my boyfriend..."

I frowned. The way she said the man's name, clearly as a nickname, made me furious over something that wasn't even mine.

"See, dear, Savannah's presence here isn't a threat to you, as you both have moved on." Mom clapped her hands.

The crease in my forehead hadn't disappeared. What the hell did moving on mean? How could I care so much about her being with another man? It's been three years; I should have forgotten her just like I forgot all my other fucks, but with Savannah, no, with her, everything had to be different.

"See you on Monday, then, Savannah. I believe by then Zachary will have gone off on some campaign trip." My mother hugged Savannah, whispering something to her.

I knew Grace was up to something. My mother always complained that she never stopped with any woman. I had achieved the status every man dreamed of, letting everyone think I was a poor guy who could have any woman he wanted without being labeled a scoundrel.

But for my family, it was time to settle down. I needed to find a woman I wanted to spend the rest of my life with, but where would I find her? It was as if I was searching in all of them for a trace of that woman from Arizona and couldn't find her because Savannah was unique, so unique that she wasn't meant to be by my side. I knew I couldn't handle the burden.

CHAPTER FIFTEEN

Savannah

I was still dazed as I left the residence, my hand cold with sweat, feeling my whole body tense. I didn't even know why I had gotten caught up in Mrs. Fitzgerald's lie. She winked at me, and before I knew it, I was already confirming it.

I didn't have a boyfriend, and I didn't understand why she wanted me to lie. I reached into my jeans pocket and grabbed the key to my truck.

Luckily, I found Michael leaning against his car. On Fridays, his shift ended earlier, but he would be back at the Fitzgerald residence early tomorrow morning.

Seeing me, he pushed off his car and came toward me, noticing my lost thoughts.

"Is everything okay, *Sav*?" he asked immediately.

"The senator is in the house," I murmured as his hand took mine.

"You're freezing, as if you've seen a ghost." He raised his hand and wiped a tear that had rolled down my cheek.

"It's probably because I saw a ghost from my past that I never wanted to see again." I bit my lip. "How can I be so stupid? He still hates me, hearing him say with all his words that I shouldn't be here. Mitch, why did I have to sleep with such an arrogant man?"

I opened my arms and threw myself into my friend's embrace. I felt his hands rubbing my back, I clung to his suit jacket, and we stayed like that for long seconds until he pulled away.

"Do you want me to give you a ride? Want to go home in my car?" he asked gently.

"No, I'll take my truck. I'm feeling better now; I've vented, and I hate the senator again." I forced a smile. Michael came closer and gave me a kiss on the forehead. "Oh, I almost forgot, I want you at my place tonight. I've invited Olivia as well."

I stepped back and headed toward my truck.

"Olivia?" He was surprised, as I didn't have many friends, only Hazel, who was above all my sister.

"Yes, I think I've made a friend." I shrugged.

Michael stopped in front of his car, accepted the invitation, and got into his vehicle. Before I got into mine, I turned around, feeling as if something was watching me, burning my back, and almost immediately regretted looking.

There he was, his eyes fixed on me as if he had witnessed the entire moment with my friend. After that, he must think we were actually dating.

Zachary Fitzgerald wanted me to be gone. He didn't deserve me, didn't deserve my gaze, didn't deserve anything from me. He had once again said he didn't want me in his life. Was it a mistake to think I could tell him about our daughter?

I turned and opened the door of my truck, easily sitting behind the wheel. My sturdy truck seemed like a beast compared to the cars that frequented that house. I started the engine without looking back at the house, even knowing his eyes were on me.

What was so wrong with me? Why did he always treat me like this? I shook my head, trying to dispel those thoughts. Nothing in my mind was worth it when it came to the senator.

WITH MY POLAROID CAMERA in hand, I took a picture of Sadie smiling as she revealed her incomplete teeth in a grin.

"Shall we have pizza night, sis?" Hazel asked as she walked into the room where I was with my daughter. "It's less work, no need to cook, and no one has to deal with the dishes afterward."

She flashed a mischievous smile.

"I think that's a great idea." I simply smiled to the side.

"You're not doing well, you can talk about it." She crossed her arms and sat down next to me on the floor.

"I ran into the senator today. What a jerk. Can you believe he'd rather I quit that job?"

"If it didn't affect our little one, I'd make that man pay in court and tarnish the Fitzgerald family. I'd love to see any of them run for president after that." Hazel got easily irritated.

Unlike me, my sister was more explosive, the type who didn't tolerate disrespect.

"Proud of my future lawyer." I raised my hand and squeezed her cheek.

"The only luck that man has is that I haven't run into him yet." Hazel flexed her arms as if showing off her muscles. "Your aunt is strong, see that, Sadie?"

"Stong, stong..." Sadie tried to imitate, making both of us laugh.

OUR DINNER WAS ENJOYABLE; Olivia met Sadie for the first time. My daughter stayed with us only briefly as she needed to stick to her usual bedtime. I didn't like disrupting her routine; it would only mess up her sleep schedule.

My aunt managed to arrive in time for dinner and had pizza with us.

I had to include my friend in the conversation because Olivia was even too shy to talk to Michael. It wasn't too difficult, though, as she was good at chatting and soon they were in a dialogue.

I still needed to talk to Michael alone since he didn't know about the lie Grace had fabricated. I really wanted my friend to get involved with Olivia; he deserved someone who had eyes only for him.

At the end of the pizza, I got up from my chair with a glass of wine in hand, clearing some plates from the table and taking them to the sink. Since Mitch was beside me, I started speaking in a whisper:

"Friend, today Mrs. Grace did something really strange; she made me lie that we were dating." Our eyes met. "I don't understand why."

"Simple, to make Zachary jealous. They want to set you two up." He leaned against the counter, and we continued talking in whispers.

"Impossible, he doesn't even like me..."

"Sav, that man is crazy about you. When we were hugging today in the parking lot, I saw him watching. Clearly, he wants you. His family knows it too. They must know that after you two were together, he couldn't stop thinking about you, and now they want to get you together." He shrugged as if stating the obvious.

"No, none of this makes sense." I shook my head vigorously.

"Trust me, it all makes sense, everything. But don't worry, we're friends, and if you went along with this lie, I'll stick with it." He winked conspiratorially.

"But what about Olivia?" I shrugged slightly.

"I'll give her a ride. Who knows..." He shrugged, making me break into a big smile.

"That's my friend." I squeezed his shoulder.

"You know, despite what happened at the beginning when I said I'd wait for you, our friendship will always be stronger. It almost feels like feelings have changed because I see you as a sister, a sister I never had." He smiled, stepping back and returning to the group conversation at the table.

That was all I wanted. Mitch's friendship; I didn't want to ruin what we had. I let out a long sigh and moved closer to the group, noticing Olivia's many glances at Michael. I guess my cupid plan worked.

CHAPTER SIXTEEN

Zachary

I had the urge to ask that driver if he was really dating my girl, which would be a tremendous mistake on my part since Savannah wasn't mine—she wasn't really anything of mine.

I should have been happy at my sister's birthday, but all the happiness drained away when I saw that girl in the hallway of my parents' house.

My bad mood was evident; everything irritated me, nothing went down well. All I could think about was the driver who had something I abandoned, someone I disregarded, someone I didn't want.

"Little brother, are you okay?" *Scar* asked, sitting next to me on Sunday morning.

"I'm fine, why wouldn't I be?" I turned my face toward her, pretending not to understand.

"I don't know, you should be more cheerful. After all, you got what you wanted—the vice-presidential candidacy alongside Chris." Scarlett was right; I should be radiant.

We had fought hard for this; our party was running for the presidency of America with one of the Fitzgeralds in the presidency again. Christopher was so wound up he wasn't even sleeping properly. Obviously, my cousin wanted this; it was his life's goal. Of the three of us, Christopher was always the most centered, the most daring.

"I'm smiling, look." I forced a smile, my sister didn't buy it, rolling her eyes.

"I know why you're like this—it's because of a blonde with blue eyes. Zach, sometimes you're so clueless," Scarlett grumbled, getting up from the couch.

I grabbed her hand, pulling her close and laying her down on the couch, doing what I always did—tickling her. *Scar* hated it.

"What am I?" I teased, hearing her loud laughter.

"Stop, Zachary, stop," she begged, unable to control her laughter.

"I'm not stopping until I repeat it and apologize afterward." Of course, I was doing it to provoke her; it was just a typical sibling relationship.

"MOMMY," my sister shouted, calling for my mother.

It wasn't long before my mother joined my father in the living room.

"Zachary, you're going to make your sister choke," was what my mother always said.

"Beg for mercy," I mocked, not taking the smile off my lips.

"I give up, I give up," Scarlett stopped laughing when I took my hands off her. I helped her up, and her brown eyes, teary from laughter, met mine. "But the fact that you're so *deadly* jealous of Savannah is..."

I made a move to grab her again, but the sly thing ran behind my father.

Scarlett was a version of my mother with brown eyes and darker hair.

"Look, girl, you're playing with danger," I mocked, sitting down on the couch and crossing my legs.

"Dear, your sister is right. You spent her entire birthday without a smile," there was my mother.

"Savannah is a thing of my past. I hope we don't talk about her anymore. Tomorrow morning, I'm going back to Washington D.C., and I hope not to hear her name again. You decided to hire the girl; now you keep her," I retorted, my bad mood returning.

"Seriously? Then why do you get so upset every time her name is mentioned?" Mom asked.

"*I don't know, I don't know*, I just want to move on with my life, pretending her existence means nothing to me," I replied, running my hand through my hair.

"Nice way to approach life." My father's authoritative tone made me look him in the eye.

"What do you want me to do? Everyone here met her, saw how sweet she is, doesn't anyone even notice that her face turns red when she's embarrassed? My routine would destroy everything perfect about that woman; she wouldn't handle it. I don't want to risk something that I know is destined to fail." I was honest about what I felt inside.

"From my time with her, I had a very different glimpse than yours. All I found was a woman who is very loving, unfiltered, extroverted, and who listens to everyone around her, Zachary. Stop thinking of Savannah as a fragile crystal because that woman can surprise you," Mom was taking the girl from Arizona's side.

"You're saying this just because you want to see me tied down."

"Yes, I do. I want my only son to be married—married for love, to a decent woman who understands that his work often requires tremendous effort from the whole family. And I see that devotion in Savannah, but the only fool who doesn't see it is you, not to call you stupid,"—at 35 years old, it was the first time my mother called me stupid, and rightly so. They were trying to make me open my eyes to something right in front of me, and only I couldn't see it.

"Anyway, she's dating the driver, isn't she?" I wanted them to say it was a lie, that the scene I saw outside on Friday was just in my head.

"Dating? No, married. There's still time to go after what's yours." Mom shrugged lightly, trying to coax me into going after the Arizona woman.

I was deep in thought. After Hanna decided to run away with her child's father, it was somewhat of a relief. I was no longer in a union, but

I couldn't tell if that relief was because I was leaving a loveless marriage or if it was because the girl I wanted at the altar wasn't Hanna.

I still keep in touch with my friend; she had a good marriage, the father of her child accepted the child, and they have an enviable union. I was even a godparent to their child.

"Savannah isn't mine," I grumbled, lost in my thoughts.

"But she could be." Dad made me look at him at that moment. "I've met the girl myself; I love talking to her. She has an aura that's missing in this family. We're always too serious, taking everything too literally. Savannah could break many stereotypes."

"Great, it seems she's won over my family." I rolled my eyes and got up from the couch. "I need to make a call to Chris and head over to William's house to discuss the new law he wants to implement here in California."

"*Oh*, son, there's one more thing," Mom called, and I looked back over my shoulder. "Savannah's resume mentioned that she has a daughter."

"A daughter? But she doesn't have any children." I was puzzled by this information.

"Yes, but she has a little girl who, from what I understand, is about to turn two..."

"Two?" I widened my eyes.

"Yes."

"No, that's impossible. There's no way she could have had a child with me. I'm sure of it." The information left me intrigued and even more tense about having Savannah back in my life.

"I didn't say the child was yours, but the ages match up quite closely. Maybe your arrogant demeanor made her feel cornered." Mom was feeding the curiosity inside me.

"If she really did that, the story would be very different." I turned and walked out of the room.

I needed to get out of that house; I needed to breathe some fresh air. I didn't even know if the child was mine, but the realization made me feel suffocated and irritated. A child? No, Savannah wouldn't be able to hide that from me—not that Savannah I met in that brief accident.

CHAPTER SIXTEEN

Savannah

I arrived a bit late at the Fitzgerald residence that morning. My little one was teething, and that made Sadie irritable. I didn't want to leave her; if I could, I'd stay with her. But besides needing to talk to her father about paternity, the money I was going to earn would help with household expenses.

Sadie cried and wanted to be held. She wanted me to stay with her, and I wanted to stay, but how could I? There's no time off for teething.

I didn't find Michael in the car he drove, nor was his vehicle there. He was probably starting work later.

Olivia confided in me via text that when Mitch dropped her off at home, there was even a kiss between them, which made me excited. My cupid plan definitely worked.

I walked through the back of the house, entering through the kitchen door. Looking around, I saw Mary enter as soon as she saw me.

"Sorry, Mary, I'm late. This morning was a mess with my little one," I said quickly.

"It's okay. Is your daughter alright?" she asked, concerned.

"Yes, her teeth are coming in, and generally, when that happens, Sadie gets a bit irritable, sometimes even with a fever."

"If you want, you can keep your phone on you today," she said, winking with concern.

"Thank you, I'll keep it with me. It will make me feel much more at ease." With a nod, I went to the bathroom to change and get ready to start working.

***

"IS SADIE DOING BETTER?" Olivia asked when we left the library.

"My aunt hasn't sent any updates. I believe everything is under control. I don't want to keep checking my phone; they might think I'm taking advantage of the situation." My colleague pushed the stroller as we talked.

"You? Really?" Olivia smiled in a teasing manner.

I rolled my eyes, knowing what it was about. The way my employers treated me was starting to spread, and now I knew the reason. Everything seemed to be getting a bit confusing in my life.

Fortunately, no one had witnessed the conversation I had with the Fitzgeralds last Friday.

"Can we talk, Miss Bellingham?" The deep voice behind us made us both turn around.

I knew who it was. I recognized that voice too well—perhaps too well.

"Can it wait, Senator?" I asked, trying to avoid him.

"It's fine, Savannah. Let me handle the stroller." Olivia wanted to help but didn't realize she was making things worse.

My eyes met the senator's, and clearly, there was no escape. I needed to have that conversation with him.

"Alright," I murmured, stepping away from Olivia as he turned towards the library we had just cleaned.

He opened the door for me, and I entered, hearing him close it behind us. We were alone inside.

I don't know how I could have thought the senator had already gone back to wherever he was staying. I stopped near one of the armchairs in the room, holding onto the back of it, keeping a good distance from Zachary.

"I thought you had gone back to Washington D.C.," I said immediately, unable to hold my tongue.

"I had to handle some matters at the State Capitol with William," he said, not taking his eyes off me. "Besides, there are other reasons..."

"Other reasons?" I interrupted, knowing he was talking about me and as always blocking his speech.

"Why are you nervous? Is there something you're hiding from me?" He tilted his head to the side.

"I'm not nervous." Obviously, I was. Everything about that man made me nervous.

"Then why are your fingers fidgeting? I'll ask again—do you have something you want to tell me?" He knew, he knew about our daughter, and he was asking already aware of the answer.

"What do you want to know?" If he knew, let him reveal it.

"About the girl who was born exactly nine months after we met, or rather, about Sadie Bellingham? That's the registered name I found when I researched her, and what's most curious is that her birth certificate doesn't have her father's name on it." Zachary knew much more than I expected.

I felt as if the ground had been taken out from under my feet, gripping the back of the chair tightly. I couldn't think or even figure out what to say.

"I... I..." I tried to speak, but nothing came out. My voice got lost somewhere inside me.

My eyes closed, and everything became blurry. The fear of losing my daughter made me faint.

I FEEL SOMETHING COLD passing over my forehead, whispered voices beside me. Slowly, I opened my eyes, focusing on the white ceiling. *Huh*, but the library ceiling isn't this color...

"Dear, are you feeling better?" I turned my face to find Grace there.

"Where am I? Where's Sadie?" I quickly sat up, putting my hand to my head with a brief dizziness.

"Calm down, you just woke up from a fainting spell," Grace placed her hand on my shoulder, and the footsteps beside me made me turn my face.

"What do you want from me?" I asked, not taking my eyes off Zachary.

"I want the truth." He was direct.

"The truth? Yes, she's your daughter. And yes, I thought about telling you many times, but I was scared, *so scared*. The words you said that night kept echoing in my mind, *I wasn't the type of woman to be by your side,* and if I wasn't, then my daughter wouldn't be either. Or if she could be and I couldn't? You can't take Sadie away from me, you can't!" Tears streamed down my face uncontrollably.

Everything became silent in the room. I had never been there, didn't know where I was. I feared for my daughter, knowing the senator might want to take her from me, and he could, after all, he had all the money, and I had nothing.

"I can't lose my little one." I began to move quickly, wanting to get out of that bed, needing to go home and run away with Sadie.

I walked towards the door but didn't get more than four steps when I felt Zachary's long fingers touch my wrist, pulling me against his chest. My face pressed into his jacket, that masculine scent hitting my senses. But I didn't have time for distractions; not even my attraction to the senator would make me lose focus on the fact that Sadie was in danger.

"Savannah! Stop, for God's sake." Zachary's voice came in a reprimand.

"You're not going to take my daughter from me..."

"No, I'm not. Will you stop trying to escape? We need to have a sensible conversation!" Holding onto his jacket tightly, I lifted my face, stopping my struggle at that moment.

"Promise you won't?" I asked, feeling exhausted from trying to fight him.

"Yes, I promise."

CHAPTER EIGHTEEN

Savannah

"I need to get back to work," I said when I was calmer, knowing I couldn't leave Olivia to handle things alone.

Mrs. Grace and her son led me to the tea room, which was more private.

"I'll ask them to replace you for today." Grace gave me a small smile.

"I need to call Christopher. He needs to know about this; after all, we're talking about his candidacy." Zachary sighed deeply, as if all this was a problem that affected them all.

Grace nodded to her son, holding my hand and guiding me into the room. I entered, looking around and finding the place clean. I dragged my hands over my service uniform, feeling them damp from the sweat of my nervousness.

"Why does Zachary need to call his cousin?" I asked fearfully, dreading the answer.

"A child during a campaign might not reflect well to voters. It's a girl who's about to turn two. Where has Zachary been during her two years of life? Why is he only discovering his paternity now? This isn't the kind of media we want at this stage. Not to mention how you'll be hounded," Grace answered calmly, trying to choose her words carefully.

"I had planned to tell him after Sadie turned two; I would have two years to prepare. It was just a time I saw as an escape valve, making my brain believe we could have made the right choice. My daughter is the most precious thing I have. I was so scared, scared that the senator would want to take her from me." I squeezed my thighs tightly, not knowing what to think from then on.

"I don't judge you, dear; I would never judge someone without knowing their side of the story. I don't know your version. All I know is what Zach has always told us about you, and I confess I'm surprised to learn that the child is his. My son has never been careless with anything." Grace gave a somewhat awkward smile.

"I didn't know how to approach the senator, and when Michael mentioned the opportunity to work here in your house, I thought it was the ideal choice, to get closer to the senator's parents, to find a way to approach him. Knowing the consequences of my actions..." My sentence trailed off when the door opened and Zachary and Arnold, his father, walked in.

"You don't need to stop talking just because I arrived," Zachary grumbled, somewhat irritated.

"My son, we need to stay calm in a moment like this," Mrs. Grace tried to smooth things over.

"A situation that could have been avoided from the start," Zachary grumbled without looking in my direction. "Isn't there any whiskey around here?"

I lifted my eyes, noticing he was looking around the room.

"There's no alcohol in this room," Grace said.

"Good." He began to walk out of the room, his steps quick, as if he could float with all his elegance.

My eyes met Mr. Arnold's; he was looking at me as if trying to unravel something.

"I'm sorry to disappoint you," I said, guessing what was on his mind.

"You haven't disappointed me; I'm just thinking about the best way to prevent this from becoming a negative public issue," it was incredible how Grace and Arnold were not against my decision.

"I... I... just didn't want to hurt you." I shrugged, looking at the floor.

"Don't think like that. You're a mother, and as a mother, I would do anything for my children. You thought this was the right thing to do, that your daughter would be safe this way. And that's okay." Grace made me lift my face towards her.

I wanted to go to that lady, throw myself into her arms, and seek comfort in her kind words. But I held back when the door opened again. Zachary entered, and at that moment, he was holding a glass of amber-colored liquid. It must have been the whiskey he had mentioned.

"Christopher asked that we make no decisions without him and our advisors present. This decision needs to be thought out; we're talking about the future of our family, about how wrong it could go if it blows up the wrong way," Zachary said without looking at me.

The room fell silent. No one spoke, but I needed to say something; I needed to know how this would affect me and my daughter.

"And what does that mean? What should I do? How will this affect my daughter and me?" I blurted out a million questions while holding my pants tightly.

"Still asking questions? It will affect everything, *damn* it! You're my mother's employee. If any employee leaks that my daughter's mother worked as a cleaner when I could provide her with a world of comfort, do you realize how much that affects everything? How broad the situation is?" Zachary stopped talking and took a sip of his whiskey.

I said nothing, remaining silent, knowing that my silence wouldn't last long, knowing I would eventually speak amid my nervousness, seeking a solution that wouldn't affect my daughter.

"Don't try to make me the only one to blame. I knew I had my share of the blame, but it wasn't just me. It wasn't only my mistake. I trusted you when you said that act wouldn't lead to anything, but it had a consequence. And know that I hid my daughter with pride, and I would hide her a million more times if necessary, to keep her from knowing an arrogant and self-important man like you!!!" My words were spat out in my fury. "Guess what? The world doesn't revolve around your belly button."

I finished speaking, catching my breath, knowing that I had finally vented a portion of everything that had been choking me inside.

Zachary looked at me with those intense eagle eyes, narrowed.

"No, you're not the only one to blame, but you are the main one," he retorted with a clenched jaw.

"Remember, it was you who wanted to do it without protection. Remember, it was you who said I wasn't the type of woman to be by your side. Remember, it was you who was about to get married. So don't put me as the main one when you were the one who started it." I began walking toward him, knowing I would poke him in the chest, fearless, with anger in my eyes.

"Enough!" Grace said loudly. "This argument will get us nowhere. Let's wait for Christopher to arrive and make the right decision. Savannah, I'll let you go home..."

"No, mother, and if she runs away with my daughter..."

"Don't call her yours, don't call her that, since you didn't even meet her!" I interrupted, growling. "My name is Savannah Bellingham, and I honor my word. I'm not like you, who always stays in line, afraid to take risks."

Mr. Arnold held his son's shoulder, restraining his impulses.

"I'm sure Savannah will honor her word. Let her go. When we call, can you come to our house? And please bring the little girl with you." I simply nodded at Mr. Arnold without looking at the senator anymore and quickly left the room, needing to get out of there, needing to breathe some fresh air.

CHAPTER NINETEEN

Savannah

I arrived at the staff parking lot and saw my friend standing next to his car. His eyes lifted in my direction, and unable to control myself, I ran toward him, once again throwing myself into his arms, letting the tears fall from my eyes.

At first, Michael said nothing. He comforted me, stroked my hair, calming me down.

"Sav, what happened? Do you want to talk to me?" he whispered in a soothing tone.

"It wasn't supposed to be like this. I shouldn't have fought with him. We needed to understand each other, for Sadie's sake, but Zachary remains the same arrogant man as always, the owner of the world; only his opinion matters." Gradually, I lifted my face. My friend wiped the tears that were running down my cheeks.

"Well, I'd like to punch him in the face, but doing that would easily cost me my job..."

"Oh, no, please don't." I shook my head, forcing a smile. "Though the image of him getting punched would be quite satisfying."

At that moment, my friend pulled me into his arms again, hugging me with affection.

"Not to mention, the senator is watching us from the window; he probably thinks I'm here comforting his woman while he plays the bitter man." I pulled my face away, looking up at Michael. "I'm not sure if it would be good for me to provoke my boss's son..."

"Should we maybe distance ourselves? I don't want this to affect your job," I said anxiously.

"Sav, nothing will push me away. Mr. Arnold knows all about this; we always have an open dialogue, and he's the one who told me to keep provoking his son. Trust me, this family wants to change their last name at all costs." He tapped the tip of his finger on my nose.

"Someone needs to tell them that to change my last name, their son would need to be born again with a genius, very, very much better." I gestured dramatically.

"That's my girl." Mitch kissed my forehead. "Are you going back to work?"

"I got the day off." I shrugged. "At least one good thing about this is that I can spend the day with my fussy teething daughter."

I smiled sincerely, remembering my little one, who I had left crying that morning because she wanted to stay with me.

"Damn, those little teeth are wearing her out." Michael grimaced.

"Too much, but first, I need to go back inside to get my clothes and change out of this one." I stepped away from Mitch, whispering to myself. "And with any luck, I won't run into that arrogant son of a bitch."

I went through the back, not wanting to run into anyone, not wanting to explain why I was leaving, not even that my daughter was the senator's. Many might call me crazy; after all, Sadie had a millionaire father, and I could benefit from all that.

But every time I remembered the arrogant way Zachary spoke to me, I remembered that this wasn't what I wanted for my little one.

I know my convictions changed after I met Grace and Arnold. They are friendly, attentive, and caring. They are helpful to all the staff; maybe Zachary treated everyone well, but that changed when it came to me.

I entered the bathroom, grabbed my clothes from the locker, and changed in one of the stalls. I let my hair down from the ponytail; I always preferred to wear it loose, but since it was one of the job rules, I kept it tied.

I put my uniform in the bag, holding it on my shoulder, not even looking at myself in the mirror, not wanting to see my red eyes.

As I left the bathroom, I bumped into Mary and Olivia, who was standing next to her.

"I hope your little one feels better," Mary said. "Mrs. Grace just mentioned that you said she had a fever. Let us know if anything changes."

I almost thanked Mrs. Grace for talking to them first and explaining what had happened.

"I hope I'm not causing any trouble," I murmured nervously.

"Never, dear, take it easy," Mary said.

I said goodbye to both of them. Olivia didn't ask any questions, which was another thing to be thankful for. I headed towards the back exit, needing to get to my truck as quickly as possible to be in the safety of my vehicle.

Michael was no longer there, and the car he was driving was gone. He must have left. I approached my truck, put the key in the lock, turning it when I heard silent footsteps behind me.

That made me quicken my pace, wanting to open the door quickly and escape from the presence of the man I knew was following me.

I opened the door, tossed my bag onto the passenger seat, and was about to get in when that warm hand covered mine as I held onto the top of the door.

"I want her back in this house within two hours." I felt his body very close to my back, his voice low as he gave the command.

"I'll be there when I want," I said without turning around. "Know that what you used to do no longer has any control over me."

"Then say that while looking into my eyes. Turn around, Savannah, turn around now!" As always, our conversations ended with him giving orders.

"No, I'm not turning around. I'm not looking into your eyes because I'm not going to risk being harshly abandoned and despised by the imposing senator." I turned around, lifted my face, and stared into his beautiful eyes.

But I didn't say what he wanted. I sighed as I looked, just to prove that I was no longer the naive girl from Arizona that Zachary once knew.

"What have I done to you?" he whispered as if to himself.

"You showed me the worst side of a man, made me hate you for treating me as just a poor, helpless girl. I have nothing more to say to you. I'll return soon with my daughter, but not at the time you specified, and at the time I choose!" I lifted my chin, pulled open my door, and got into my truck, slamming the door shut behind me.

I might have been wrong, I might have hidden our daughter from him, but one thing I learned from Zachary Fitzgerald: if I kept my guard down and showed him my sweetest side, that man would think he could dominate me, that I would be his puppet, but that was never going to happen.

I drove away, revving my monstrous engine, not looking at the senator who was still standing there, glaring at me.

Alone, leaving the Fitzgerald house, I allowed myself to slump my shoulders and cry, cry alone before showing strength in front of others.

CHAPTER TWENTY

Savannah

"I'm not letting you go alone into that den of snakes," Hazel said immediately when I told her I needed to return to the Fitzgerald house.

"Sister, you can't go there calling them that, although some do deserve it. But Mrs. Grace and Mr. Arnold are good people." My daughter held up a doll, extending it towards me. "Shall we play, my dear?"

"Yes, yes, yes." She flashed a big smile, showing her lovely little teeth.

"I'll control myself, I promise. But you can't go alone; you need a lawyer by your side." She crossed her arms, looking at me seriously.

Hazel was very much like me, the only difference being that her hair was a shade of light brown, while mine was blonde. My sister was 20 years old, and I was 25.

"Don't forget that you're only in your second year of college," my aunt said with a smile.

"A half-lawyer, alright?" Hazel walked over to my daughter, crouching down and gently stroking her blonde hair. "Auntie will show what the Bellinghams are capable of."

She winked, and Sadie clapped her hands, not understanding anything that her aunt had said.

"The senator said to come in two hours, but I don't want to do his bidding. I'll go only when it gets dark, by which time I'm sure many of the staff won't be there anymore," I said, mimicking a mother rocking her child to sleep, watching Sadie stand up and put the toy bottle in the doll's mouth.

"Perfect. That senator needs to know that it's the Bellinghams who are in charge." I flashed a big smile at my sister's conviction.

"Hazel, you make it seem like we're going to war," I teased.

"If you think it's better, we can go armed with our pistols. We could turn it into a western movie, the girls from Arizona against the world." Hazel made a gesture with her hand as if pulling an imaginary gun from her holster.

"Your vivid imagination cracks me up." What was supposed to be a serious conversation turned into a joke, and soon we were laughing and playing with Sadie.

There was no bad time that couldn't end with a good dose of humor.

I ENTERED THE BACK of the house, the same route I took when coming to work. I wasn't sure if I could enter through the front door; I didn't know how to behave not being a housekeeper there.

I turned off the car and looked over at Hazel, who was admiring everything.

"This is just the staff area, right?" she asked, knowing that I had mentioned it to her.

"Yes, it's beautiful, isn't it?"

"Beautiful would be an understatement for all this," she murmured, still admiring.

I shook my head, opened my door, walked around the car, and took my little one from my sister's arms. We were both dressed similarly, in a flowery dress and little boots. It was all we usually wore.

I hugged my little one to my chest, as if afraid someone might take her from me, the fear overtaking me every time that thought crossed my mind.

We moved in silence to the back entrance, avoiding the kitchen area, and I saw the door to the living room open. It was Mary, who greeted us with a smile. I approached her, with my daughter hugging me tighter, her little face pressed against my neck, feeling shy.

"Hello, dear. Mrs. Grace told me everything. You can rest assured that your secret is safe with me. I just continued the lie because Olivia likes to talk and sometimes says too much," Mary said, and I nodded, knowing it was true.

"This is my sister Hazel. She came to be my lawyer," I whispered with a smirking smile.

"A half-lawyer is better than none," Hazel shrugged.

Mary nodded for us to follow her. Being there in that house with Sadie in my arms made everything feel more real. I was about to introduce my little one to her father's family and to her father himself.

From the corner of my eye, I noticed that Hazel was controlling herself just like I was, trying not to crack one of her out-of-place jokes. I had fully adjusted to that luxurious environment, unlike Hazel, who was still admiring everything.

The housekeeper guided us to the center of the room. Sadie didn't recognize the unfamiliar environment, so she remained hiding her face in my neck.

I raised my eyes when I thought I would only find the senator and his parents there, but no. Also present were the presidential candidate Christopher Fitzgerald, the Governor of California William Fitzgerald, and several other men, whom I could bet were the fathers of the other two men. My God, I didn't expect to encounter such a large number of Fitzgeralds together.

"I told you it was a conspiracy, little sister," Hazel jabbed me, whispering at my side.

"Dear, it's great that you've arrived and with company." Mrs. Grace rose from the sofa, always being a wonderful hostess.

"This is my sister Hazel," I said to her.

"The one studying law," Grace remarked to Hazel.

"And who is already ready to represent the family," Hazel, like me, had no limit to what she said when nervous.

"I imagine so." Mrs. Grace smiled, giving a brief kiss on my sister's cheek before turning back to me. "Is she asleep?"

"Oh, she's just shy. New environment, new people." I pouted, trying to smile.

I still hadn't looked at the senator. I didn't know how to face him with our daughter in my arms.

"I think it's best to let her get used to the environment while I introduce you," Mrs. Grace said, asking us to follow her closer to the guests. "These are Savannah and Hazel Bellingham, and this little one is my granddaughter, Sadie."

Hearing Grace refer to Sadie as her granddaughter made me seek Zachary's gaze, finding it fixed on me with no expression. His hands in his pockets made me think he was clenching them. Grace introduced everyone, and all I could manage to say in response was a distracted "uh-huh," losing focus on the introductions as I was trapped in an imaginary bubble where only Zachary and I existed, the man I swore to hate.

CHAPTER TWENTY-ONE

Zachary

There she was, standing in the center of my parents' living room, with that tiny, wonderful little thing in her arms. It was as if my eyes were glued to the scene, Savannah holding my daughter.

What did I miss? How must Savannah have felt when she was carrying our daughter? What was it like to hear her first cries in the world? Her first smiles, her first word, crawling, first steps...

I missed all of that. I missed a part of my daughter's life. And the only one to blame was me, all because I unloaded all my emotional baggage onto that woman, spewing how she wasn't good enough to be by my side.

I held Savannah's gaze, wanting to be there with her, to hold her hand, but I knew none of that was possible. There was no way to make up for my mistake.

"Can we be brief with this matter?" Christopher broke my fixation on the woman, looking at my cousin who was trying to control himself, searching for a solution to my problem.

"Son, we can't put the cart before the horses," my Aunt Natalie, Chris's mother, said, trying to calm her son.

"I'm calm, Mom, very calm," Christopher directed his eyes toward me, narrowing them.

"We all understand the risk we're facing. It's the first time one of our boys is running for the presidency, and we need to find a solution so that no one is negatively affected," my father tried to be sensible, always leading, looking at Chris's advisor. "Do you have any ideas?"

"One idea I had was for the child's mother to come forward and talk about the paternity, speak the truth. What's the problem with that? Zachary can play the role of the devastated father who didn't know he had a daughter..."

"And my sister gets to be the villain? Rest assured, if she goes public, it won't just be her image that will be tarnished but also that of your future president." The girl next to Savannah had a sweet and innocent look, but as soon as she spoke, she revealed the exact opposite.

She even glared at Christopher, her eyes filled with fury. From what I gathered, her name was Hazel, and she was studying law, which meant she understood a bit about the subject. It was as if my Savannah was her client, and this wasn't supposed to be a trial.

"I could withdraw my candidacy for vice-president..."

"No! I need you exactly by my side," Christopher growled at me.

"I thought you wanted me dead," I grumbled, irritated.

"And I still do. It was obvious that all your debauchery would end in an unwanted pregnancy. I told you, Zachary, don't go out with anyone, don't think only about sex!" Christopher had his eyes fixed on me.

"That's easy for you to say, the imprisoned widower," I retorted.

"Easy? Bury the love of your life and then come tell me it's easy." My cousin didn't even get up from the sofa. He was losing his patience but not his composure.

"Arguing won't solve our problems," Uncle Carter, Christopher's father, said.

Natalie and Carter lived in Washington D.C. with their son, having moved there due to the elections. We had houses all over the United States, so moving was easy. With the news of my fatherhood, they came along with their son, so they could meet everyone.

My Uncle Edward and Aunt Abigail, William's parents, lived in Sacramento, California, close to my parents.

"Well, can we wait to announce until after the elections?" Christopher's advisor spoke up after a long silence.

"The elections are in eight months! I'll have to stay away from my daughter for another eight months? No, that option is out of the question," I was harsh about that.

"Zach is right. We're talking about a child, his own blood," William took my side.

"I agree. If it were my child, I wouldn't want to be away from him for any longer," my two cousins stood by me.

The Fitzgeralds were very close-knit; no matter the occasion, we stood side by side.

"Not necessarily do you need to stay apart..."

"And risk being discovered, with the weaker side being blamed?" Once again, Savannah's sister spoke, and I could see that she received a nudge from her sister.

The two of them were very similar, but it was clear that Hazel was younger, with darker hair than her sister. Even their outfits were similar.

"There is a solution that would be beneficial for everyone, but it requires a drastic change," the advisor seemed to not care about Hazel's interruptions, unlike Christopher, who was obsessed with control and hated when people interrupted him. He was a good man but impatient and somewhat perfectionist.

"Just tell us what the solution is," I asked, anxious.

"In a statement, we announce that the senator has rekindled a great love from the past, and from that love, he learned that she had a daughter. Therefore, he decided not to waste any more time and marry his beloved." I widened my eyes.

There was a sigh of relief from the women in my family; they seemed to like that fairy tale. But all I could do was look at my Savannah, noticing she had her eyes on me. The little one was still hiding her face on her mother's neck. My anxiety to see her face was starting to make me euphoric inside.

"Are you talking about a wedding?" Mom broke the silence.

"Yes, voters love that romantic, perfect family atmosphere..." The advisor let the sentence trail off, as if leaving the rest to our imagination.

"But for that to happen, there needs to be a bride who agrees to this crazy plan," Savannah spoke up for the first time.

"Dear." My mother looked at Savannah as if begging her to accept it.

"There's no way this can happen. Savannah already has a boyfriend," I shrugged.

"Relationships can be broken," Aunt Natalie joined in favor of the crazy plan.

"That wasn't in my plans. Besides, the senator has made it clear that I'm not the type of woman to be by his side." Savannah's hurt eyes met mine.

"You're always going to throw that in my face, aren't you?" I grumbled.

"Until my last breath." She shrugged as if taunting me.

It was clear that she still felt the same way I did, but she wouldn't back down.

"And if I retract everything I said, would you marry me, for the sake of our daughter, so she isn't harshly exposed?" I started to play on the side I knew would affect her, which wasn't very honest of me.

Savannah didn't say anything, looked at her sister, both exchanging a glance as if speaking to each other. Everyone fell silent, waiting for the woman's response, until she sighed and began to speak:

"Fine, but with my conditions. It will be a marriage for Sadie's sake. We'll sleep in separate beds, I don't want any contact with you. We'll pretend to be husband and wife, but within our privacy, we'll be just two strangers. And also, the engagement announcement will only happen after you ask my father for my hand in marriage."

"This must be a joke," I muttered.

"Family traditions." She shrugged.

"Yes, he will ask," William answered for me. "Brother, she's agreeing. It shouldn't be too difficult to ask her father for her hand in marriage."

"Great." I rolled my eyes.

"Can your parents come to Sacramento, dear?" Mom asked.

"I'll talk to them," Savannah replied.

The strangest part of all this was that Savannah didn't even care about having a boyfriend, which made me think there wasn't a relationship, but there was still a man who kept touching the woman who should only be touched by me.

CHAPTER TWENTY-TWO

Savannah

I turned my face; Sadie still kept her little face nestled against my neck, her tiny hands gripping the fabric of my shirt tightly.

"My little one," I called her affectionately.

Sadie merely wiggled her face, smiling in her shy way.

"There are people here who want to meet you," I whispered, stroking her back, hoping my daughter would feel comfortable enough to lift her face.

Slowly, Sadie lifted her face, her little hand gripping the nape of my neck with a firm hold.

Grace approached us, clearly excited to see her granddaughter. In contrast, Zachary seemed to be in a trance.

"Hello," Grace said gracefully beside Sadie. "You're a very pretty girl, you know that?"

My daughter gave a shy smile, shaking her head and then placing it back against my neck.

"Sadie isn't used to new environments, and it's making her feel shy," I explained to Grace.

"That's alright, I believe I can win this little lady's trust." Grace gently stroked my daughter's back, who once again lifted her face.

"If you have cookies, you might win her over with her stomach," Hazel said, and out of the corner of my eye, I saw my sister handing one of the cookies I made for Sadie to Grace.

"Great idea." Grace accepted the cookie and looked back at my daughter. "Look, Sadie, what I have here. Want a piece?"

"Yes," Sadie responded quickly, moving to the floor.

"That easy?" Grace flashed a victorious smile.

"Let's just say it was the right strategy," Hazel said, putting the remaining cookies into the paper bag and placing it in her purse.

"I hadn't thought to bring the cookies," I thanked my sister.

"You've gotten this girl used to only homemade food; we need to be prepared." Hazel shrugged.

"Do you make these cookies?" Grace asked.

"Oh, yes, I do..."

"Savannah has a phobia that canned foods or any other derivatives might contain some bacteria." Hazel rolled her eyes.

"Better safe than sorry, and I spent most of my time with her; I enjoyed making a mess with Sadie."

"One day I came home from college and thought Sadie had turned into a little ghost," Hazel teased, breaking into a big smile.

"That's because my helper accidentally knocked a bag of flour on her head; we spent a week getting flour out of her ear." Remembering that day was funny, now that it was over.

"You must be an amazing mother to my granddaughter." Grace bent down beside Sadie, who was eating her cookie as if it were the last sweet on earth.

"She's everything I have that's good," I said with my face lowered.

Grace looked at my daughter with affection; it was clear how warmly they accepted her, without even asking for a paternity test. Mr. Arnold approached, his eyes fixed on my little one.

"She reminds me so much of Zachary when he was a baby; even the shape of her mouth is the same," which couldn't be denied, it was the same shape as her father's.

Arnold crouched beside his wife.

"Hello, sweetie." Arnold extended his hand.

Sadie gave a shy smile, her little hands covered in crumbs, looking at his hand. She lifted her hand, placing it on top of his, taking two steps closer to them.

"What?" She offered the remaining cookie crumbs. "I'm done..." She brought it to her mouth, eating the rest with a little show.

"That's it, girl," Hazel said proudly.

"You only teach her things she shouldn't learn," I grumbled.

But Sadie didn't move away from them, holding her dirty hand over her grandfather's.

"Wow, she made a huge mess with just one cookie," I said, looking at the floor.

"That's alright. Sadie can turn this house upside down and it won't be a problem." Arnold easily picked up the little one and held her in his lap, Grace standing beside him.

Soon, everyone was gathered around my daughter, fawning over her, and Sadie, who had moved past her shyness, was amazed by all the attention. Were all of Zachary's relatives here exclusively to meet the new family member?

"Sav, are you really going to go through with this marriage?" my sister asked.

"Do I have a better option? We're talking about Sadie here. I can't risk her pictures being splashed across every magazine as the senator's hidden daughter and me as the neglectful mother," I whispered back.

"We both know you're not neglectful," she murmured.

"I've accepted this crazy deal; now I'll face my responsibilities. I'm not going to risk a legal battle. I don't want to risk having Sadie away from me, so I'm going along with it." I spoke seriously.

"Alright, but I'll tell you one thing: Dad is going to freak out. He'll want to know every detail, and if he finds out this marriage isn't for the right reasons, he'll be against it," Hazel's words only confirmed what I had already suspected.

"Zachary will have to pretend it's real." I shrugged.

"That's the least of it. The man hasn't taken his eyes off you for a single minute, and when he did, it was to look at Sadie. It's clear he cares about her much more than a mere contract," Hazel teased me.

"And you should stop interrupting the poor assistant; the future president looked like he was going to kill you," I widened my eyes at her.

"That widower needs a good fuck to get the bitterness out of his voice." I poked my sister, who covered her mouth to stifle a loud laugh.

"Hazel!" I scolded.

"Sister, sorry, but oh, that man with the bitter look..." she glanced quickly at the future president. "He's hot, really hot. In person, they're even more intense..."

Hazel avoided another poke by stepping back. We were speaking in whispers, so we weren't overheard.

I turned my gaze back to Zachary, who at that moment seemed to be walking in my direction. I swallowed hard; I would have to get used to being by his side. I needed to adapt to the fact that we were going to share the same house solely for the sake of our daughter and the elections.

Yes, those were the reasons—nothing more.

CHAPTER TWENTY-THREE

Zachary

I approached Savannah slowly, unsure of how to act around her. I wanted to go to my daughter, hold her in my arms, and promise that I would never be absent from her life again. But I didn't know how to do it. I never thought I'd be in such a situation; I had prepared for everything in life except being in the presence of my daughter.

A little piece of me, *our*.

"How do you do it?" was the first thing I asked as I stopped beside Savannah.

I lowered my face to meet those clear, beautiful eyes.

"Do what?" she asked, her eyebrow arching slightly in a humorous way.

"To be with her? How can I hold her? I don't even know how to approach her..." I began to feel embarrassed, talking about a little girl.

"Well, you can start by doing what everyone else does—just approach her." She shrugged, and I could see that Savannah was trying hard not to laugh at me.

"There are too many people around her." I pouted.

"Then I can't help you." Savannah bit the corner of her lip and began to ignore me.

I had the chance to have everything with her, and I squandered it. Now I would face the consequences, reaping the fruits of my actions, tinged with the anger of the woman from Arizona.

"Yeah, I deserve this," I grumbled, putting my hand in my dress pants pocket, watching the little girl from a distance.

William, who had been unusually quiet, approached. My cousin, the Governor of California, was a man of few words, often serious. He and Christopher were quite similar in temperament, though in terms of physical appearance, Christopher was the most different.

"Brother, you know she's just a little girl, right?" William said, without regard for Savannah standing next to him.

"Screw you," I muttered irritably.

"When do you plan to talk to her father?" William, ever the practical one, asked.

I turned my gaze to Savannah, who had overheard our conversation.

"I'll call him tomorrow morning..."

"Would it be better if we went to see him?" I asked, feeling anxious about it.

"It's better not to." Savannah's pursed lips made me realize there was a reason behind it.

"And what would that reason be?" I asked, frowning.

"Well, this is outside his usual environment, you know..."

"No, I don't know." I crossed my arms, looking seriously at Savannah.

"What she means is that my father carries a weapon; he wouldn't hesitate to use it if he knew your marriage wasn't for love. You know, Dad is very protective," Hazel, who was next to my mother, chimed in, bringing our conversation to everyone present.

"What are you talking about?" I turned my gaze back to Savannah, after all, it was her hand I would be asking in marriage.

"My father believes in marriages for love; he married my mother because he loved her unconditionally. He would never accept me marrying someone I don't love. But it shouldn't be too hard for you, you know... *to lie.*" Savannah shrugged.

"I'm not used to lying," I retorted.

"Funny, you lied the first time we met..."

"No, I didn't lie; I just omitted a fact," I cut her off, getting irritated.

"A very important fact. Lucky was the woman who ran away. *Great*, I, who hate scandals, am about to marry a woman with absolutely no boundaries."

"No, I'm not going to entertain this topic," I grumbled, running my hand through my hair.

I turned my back on Savannah, leaving her to talk to herself. I'm good at that—ignoring people. I walked to the bar area of my father's place, grabbed a glass, and then one of the whiskey bottles, filling it with the amber liquid. Beside me, I noticed my cousin Christopher joining, asking me to fill a glass for him.

"I hope this marriage doesn't ruin our campaign," Chris grumbled, taking the full glass and bringing it to his mouth.

"It won't. I won't let it," I said firmly.

"We'll see about that." Christopher turned to look at the guests. "And doesn't the little girl look just like you?"

I stepped out from behind the bar, standing next to him, and looked at the little girl.

"I don't know how to approach her. What if she cries? What if she doesn't like me?" The questions were so numerous that they even kept me from getting closer to her.

"Brother, we're talking about a nearly two-year-old girl. It shouldn't be that hard. Just go," I felt his hand touch my shoulder.

"How many children do you have again?" I turned my face to him.

"Unfortunately, none. But if I had any, I wouldn't be doing this indecisive man's job." He rolled his eyes next to me.

"It's not as easy as it seems." Actually, it is easy.

My subconscious was making everything difficult. Knowing that this little girl was mine, that I was her father, it felt like a new feeling was budding inside me—something akin to overprotectiveness, taking over my heart without even speaking to me.

How could I live in a world capable of doing harm to that little one? How could I share her with others when all I wanted was to keep her in the comfort of my arms, so no harm would come to her?

"Just make it easy. Let the girl into your life." I turned my face away from my little daughter, looking at my cousin.

He was right; it simply depended on me. I needed and wanted to be Sadie's father. I had spent too much time away from her to waste it now.

Without saying another word, I left my glass on the bar counter and walked towards my mother, who was with Sadie at that moment. My confident steps turned hesitant as I approached them. Mom saw me coming, smiled, and turned my daughter towards me.

This was the first time I saw her up close. Her blue eyes met mine, her short blonde hair—she didn't have much hair yet. She was simply the most beautiful child I had ever seen.

"What should I do?" I whispered, unprepared for that moment.

"Just be her father. It's not that hard," Dad said beside me.

I grew up watching Scarlett go through all the stages of childhood. I knew how to hold a child, but this one was mine. I wanted to be the best for Sadie, and I would be.

CHAPTER TWENTY-FOUR

Savannah

I could confess that I was even getting emotional seeing Zachary approaching Sadie, if it weren't for my daughter making a small pout, her eyes filling with tears—she was about to cry.

Seeing the situation, I approached them, not sure if the crying was due to Zachary's approach, or if it was just because of a new man in the little one's life, not to mention the two new teeth coming in at the same time.

My daughter saw me coming, stretched her little arms in my direction, tears already starting to roll down her cheeks.

"Oh, my little one." I extended my arms to her, and she quickly hugged my neck.

I recognized my daughter's cries and knew it wasn't because of Zachary's approach, but because of her teething.

I turned to my sister, who had come with Sadie's bag, knowing it contained a cream to relieve the pain.

"Is she okay?" the senator asked, looking genuinely concerned.

"Yes, she's fine. It's her teeth," I said without looking at Zachary. "I need to go to the kitchen to wash my hands."

"I'll come with you." Zachary acted quickly.

"I know where it is," I muttered.

"Still, I'll come." I rolled my eyes, heading to the kitchen with his footsteps close behind.

I entered the room where the cooks were preparing dinner. I didn't know why I was still surprised by this; the Fitzgeralds didn't use the kitchen themselves—others prepared their meals.

"Let's go, it's better in the bathroom," Zachary said in a not very loud tone, gesturing for me to follow, which I did.

We didn't go upstairs; we went to the family-only powder room. I hadn't even entered it during all the days I worked there.

The senator opened the door, and I entered with my daughter. He went to the sink. Seeing that Sadie was calmer, I said:

"Can you hold her for a bit?"

"Me?" The way the senator said it was somewhat comical.

"Is there someone else here?" I needed to add a bit of humor to the situation.

"But she cried when I approached." Zachary was hesitant.

"It wasn't because of you; it's her teeth. Come on, hold her," I asked, knowing the senator wanted to but was feeling uneasy.

Zachary approached and carefully held Sadie's little body. Our daughter turned towards her father. It was easier than I expected. He knew how to hold the girl; he had a natural way with her.

"See, it didn't hurt," I whispered, moving closer to the sink, leaving the cream there while I washed my hands so I could put my finger in Sadie's mouth and apply the cream.

"Aren't you afraid?" Zachary asked, seeming to reflect internally on something.

"I've been afraid since the day I found out she was inside me. I was even more scared when I heard her first cry. I'm still afraid, afraid of what the world might do to our little girl, but it all pays off when I wake up every day next to her, hearing her sweet voice calling me 'Mommy.' Every risk is worth it when I see her. I love my daughter like I've never loved anything else in this life, and I would do anything for her safety," I concluded, turning off the faucet and facing both of them.

"Daddy..." Sadie began to stroke her father's face, running her hand through his beard.

"She's having fun with your beard," I teased, moving closer to them and seeing Zachary with his eyes fixed on our daughter.

I put a small amount of cream on my finger.

"Look at Mommy," I asked, with Sadie looking at me.

I rubbed my finger between her little teeth, going to where the canine tooth was cutting through, and applied the cream. Then I did the same on the other side of her gums, with Zachary watching the whole time.

"Doesn't she mind this?" he asked, curious.

"No, this cream relieves the pain; it sort of numbs it," I finished applying it, washing my hands again, and then turning to them.

"And what about your boyfriend? He agreed to marry me even though he has a boyfriend? I feel like this story is very poorly told," he said, frowning, without even handing Sadie back to me, who was still fascinated with his beard.

I let out a long sigh, knowing I had to tell the truth. And I might need to do it sooner rather than later, or he might think I was being like him—a traitor.

"I don't have a boyfriend; that story was made up by Grace, and I just went along with it. Michael is just my friend, my best friend, the man who stood by me when you said I wasn't good enough to be by your side." This story always irritated me.

Zachary muttered something I didn't understand, as if he were cursing and didn't want our daughter to hear.

"That's just like my mother," was all he said, turning his back without letting go of Sadie, heading to the living room with her.

I had to quicken my pace to catch up with him. Zachary had closed himself off in such a way that I couldn't understand the reason. As I approached the other guests, I saw my sister talking with Mrs. Natalie, Christopher's mother. Grace introduced all the family members, and surprisingly, they were not at all snobbish despite the amount of money they had.

I moved closer to my sister, but kept my eyes on Zachary the whole time. I should let them get to know each other, but I admitted to feeling a small pang of jealousy for not being able to be there with them. It should be a moment for them. They needed to get to know each other. My daughter deserved a father who loved her as much as I did.

"Know that if you want to intern at our office, this is my number," Mrs. Natalie seemed to be handing her phone to my sister.

"What are you talking about?" I asked, momentarily distracted from the fact that my little one was with her father.

"Isn't it amazing? Mrs. Natalie said they're always recruiting new interns at their law firm." My sister had a huge smile on her face.

"And why haven't you accepted yet?" I inquired, intrigued.

"I can't intern in my field for now." She shrugged a little.

"But if you want, there's a position to be my assistant. Carter and I are always in the office, but obviously, you'll need to be around me more. Mrs. Natalie made the suggestion to my sister. "It may seem crazy since we've just met, but I liked your attitude. I believe the world needs more fearless people. We have a large firm, but you would need to move to Washington D.C. However, that might not be a problem since your sister will need to move there if Christopher wins the election, and we have good colleges around the area."

"I'll need to move?" I interjected.

"Yes, wasn't it mentioned? The Vice-President has a permanent residence in Washington D.C.," Mrs. Natalie looked at me as if it were no big deal.

But to me, it was. Chasing Zachary wherever he went was much more than I had anticipated.

CHAPTER TWENTY-FIVE

Savannah

"I'll accompany you to the car," Zachary offered, even though it wasn't necessary.

"We know how to go on our own," I grumbled irritably.

It seemed that the need to move to a new city almost immediately didn't sit well with me.

"In any case, I'm going. It's a matter of good manners," the senator said.

"Such courtesy," I muttered again.

Sadie was sleeping in my lap, her little hand resting on the fabric of my dress. Most of the Fitzgeralds had already gone to their homes, including those who lived out of state but also had a house in the city.

"Let me drive, sister," Hazel said, and I nodded because I didn't want to pass Sadie from my arms, which might wake her.

My sister moved a step ahead, and I stayed a little behind as the senator stopped beside me.

"I need to know when you'll call your father; I have to make arrangements," he said.

"I'll call him tomorrow morning," I said softly so as not to wake Sadie.

"Great, I'll arrange for one of our jets to be available so you can get here as quickly as possible." At that moment, I turned to look at the senator, not understanding his urgency.

"Can I know the reason for your hurry?" I raised my eyebrow, stopping my walk and letting Hazel get to the car first.

"To not be further away from you two. I've spent too much time away from my daughter to waste any more," he initially spoke in plural, then referred only to our daughter, which confused me, a confusion that probably shouldn't exist, since I was convinced I needed to ignore him and continue hating him.

"Only for her. Don't include me in your plans," I said, turning back to the car when I felt his hand on my shoulder, making me look back at him over my shoulder.

"Savannah, before we get married, we need to talk privately. We're not entering into a simple agreement; this is a marriage, something that needs to last for many years without an expiration date. Above all, it's essential to have a partnership, a friendship, perhaps..."

"I don't make friends with lying men who use women and then abandon them." I was firm, pouring out all my bitterness from that day and our first time.

"Alright, I deserve that," the man huffed, closing his eyes as if trying to control himself.

"We'll have all that you mentioned, but outside the house where we'll live. Inside, until Sadie becomes aware of her surroundings, we'll be strangers—a man I have no desire to get to know." I freed myself from him and walked back to the car where my sister was already waiting.

Hazel leaned over the seat, opening the door for me. I got in without difficulty, and as soon as the car started, I only realized I had been holding my breath once we had definitely left the Fitzgeralds' house.

When I exhaled, I felt the lump forming in my throat, tears welling up in my eyes. I turned to my sister.

"What am I doing, Hazel? Am I really going to marry the man who only wanted me for a casual fling?" I bit my lip, stifling my sniffles.

"It seems so. I know you're doing this for our little one. I understand your fear, and I share it, since you hid the paternity, and they have enough money to take her away from us. Know that I support you in everything, and if necessary, I'll follow you to Washington D.C." She gave me one of her sincere smiles.

"It will work out; after all, it's just a fake marriage," I whispered, using one of my free hands to wipe under my nose.

"A marriage in which you'll have to live under the same roof as him and still pretend to love him in front of everyone. And let's face it, you'll be forgiven if you can't resist that man's magnetism." Hazel made a joke that made me laugh silently so as not to wake my little one.

Soon the tears subsided, and I managed to focus more on what we were discussing.

OF ALL THE DIFFICULT things I've done in my life, telling my father that I was getting married on such short notice was by far the most distressing, especially over the phone. Dad almost had a meltdown.

It took Mom's help to calm him down.

What made the situation a little worse was when I said it was with Sadie's father. Dad flipped out, shouted, and asked if everything was okay, if I was being blackmailed. Obviously, that wasn't the case, but it was all about financial matters, and I knew I had done wrong by hiding Zachary's paternity.

When I mentioned my future husband's name, I thought the situation might improve since Dad had always liked the Fitzgeralds politically. But it got worse; he concluded that I was crazy and must be marrying on a whim.

Even before ending the call, he and Mom were already packing their bags. Mr. Peter would never let one of his daughters marry without the groom first asking for her hand in marriage and passing the loyalty test that his eyes evaluated.

When I ended the call, my hands were sweating, and fear and anguish took over me. My father didn't even accept the Fitzgeralds' jet and said he would never board a "metal bird." This meant I had about thirteen hours to prepare myself psychologically, the time it took to travel from our city in Arizona to Sacramento.

Receiving Mary's message that morning made it clear what I had already suspected: Grace had talked to her, inventing a story about Sadie, making it seem like she would stay home with my daughter. Mary just sent me a message wishing my daughter well and advised me to take that time to focus on her without worry.

Obviously, I wouldn't be working at Grace's house anymore. The Fitzgeralds didn't want it spread around that the senator's prospective bride was their maid.

Spending the day with all that anxiety was far from relaxing. What would my father say to Zachary? Would he approve of the marriage? And if, by chance, Dad refused and was against it? What would I do with my daughter?

With these thoughts came all the tremors of losing my little one.

CHAPTER TWENTY-SIX

Savannah

My father's arrival filled me with joy; seeing Dad and Mom made my heart beat with comfort, the two people who made me feel the safest in my entire life.

Although I knew that our meeting was under less than comfortable circumstances. At first, we just hugged, catching up as if there were no real reason for them to be there.

We had a breakfast full of conversation in the typical Bellingham style; Dad and Mom were exhausted from the trip, having spent a long time driving in their truck, arriving early that morning.

Dad wanted to go to the Fitzgeralds' house right away, but he was gently forced to go to sleep, being pushed by my mother and his sister, my aunt.

What made me more anxious was the fact that he wasn't talking about the issue with me, as if he wanted to discuss it with the senator first. Peter was a playful man with everyone, but when it came to his daughters, he became very protective.

I STOPPED IN FRONT of the mirror; I shouldn't be worrying about what kind of dress I was wearing, but curiously, I wanted to look pretty.

"How do I look?" I asked, standing there in that light floral dress. It was a dress in light shades, with no flashy details, a square neckline that didn't reveal much.

"Sister, you could wear a clown costume and still look beautiful." Hazel turned on my bed, lying on her back.

"I haven't worn these sandals in so long I'm afraid the sole might come off," I muttered, looking at my medium heels.

"If you want, you can borrow one of mine, though they're probably just as old as yours. We're Arizona girls, we love our boots." She winked playfully.

"I wish it were today; I like having someone to run to when things go wrong." I gave a crooked smile.

"I wish I could see Dad scare the senator, but I really need to study for the test tomorrow, especially if I'm considering the possibility of moving to Washington D.C." Her eyes sparkled at the thought.

"You want that, don't you?" I asked, curious.

"You know, Mrs. Natalie Fitzgerald was always my childhood dream, so elegant, always impeccable. And she studied law just like I did. Of course, I'm nothing like her," she concluded, sitting up on the bed, "but you know, I could work with her, become a more polished woman..."

"Hazel, I like you as you are. I'm not fond of the idea of changing you," I cut in, not liking the direction of the conversation.

"Sister, it's just a figure of speech." Hazel shrugged, seeming to want to change the subject. "Are you sure you're comfortable in those sandals?"

"Don't I look like I am?" I murmured, confused.

"Actually, you look great, the perfect vision of a senator's future wife." She gave a huge smile.

"Oh, that topic gives me chills and shivers." I made a face, hearing my sister's laughter.

I picked up my phone from the dresser, then my daughter's bag, who was sleeping with me in the same room, and said goodbye to Hazel with a kiss on her cheek before leaving the room.

Sadie was with her grandparents catching up, they wouldn't even let me get near my daughter, saying it was their time.

I approached the living room, my steps echoing. The first to look up was Dad, who scanned my outfit with a critical eye.

"No boots?" He raised an eyebrow.

"An Arizona woman doesn't lose her roots just because she's without her boots," I said reflectively.

"I like it." Dad smiled, getting up from the sofa and picking up my little one. "It looks like we're going to meet your father, and they didn't even let me bring my pistol. I just wanted to scare the senator..."

"I've been married to you for over 27 years, long enough to know that you wouldn't just scare him if you had your pistol," Mom retorted, making Dad roll his eyes.

We went outside, my aunt coming along, all of us in Dad's double-cab truck. I sat in the back seat with my daughter. Sadie was noisily gnawing on a toy, as if her teeth were bothering her so much she wanted to destroy it.

"You know what's stranger?" Dad said while driving, following the GPS route on his dashboard control.

"What, Dad?" I knew that question was for me.

"For a woman in love, you've said very little about your fiancé." He looked at me through the rearview mirror, trying to gauge my reactions.

"That's out of fear, fear of what you'll think of him. This is the first time I'm introducing a man to you formally, and my father is wanting to bring a pistol." I didn't divert my gaze, knowing that any deviation would make Peter think I was bluffing and lying.

Dad fell silent, and we continued on our way to the Fitzgeralds' house.

DAD PARKED THE TRUCK in front of the Fitzgeralds' house. They were already aware we were coming since I had messaged Grace; she was the one who contacted me, not her son.

I got out of the car and kept my little one in my arms, giving me a reason to cling to something.

"Wow, this looks like one of those mansions from the soap operas you watch, dear," Dad said to Mom, holding her hand.

My father was a stark contrast in that residence, wearing his cowboy boots, jeans, and a plaid shirt under his leather jacket. It was the lightest jacket he had, so it wouldn't soak up too much sweat.

We approached the door, which was immediately opened by Mary. I believed she was the only staff member who knew about my connection with the Fitzgeralds.

"Welcome, everyone. I'll show you to the living room." Mary winked at me.

Dad whispered some of his jokes to Mom, who poked him to be quiet. I loved their dynamic; no matter how many years passed, they always kept the same quirks.

We entered the living room, where I found only Mr. Arnold and Grace. Obviously, Dad rubbed his hand on his pants; he was nervous.

Dad was a big fan of Arnold; he was one of the most beloved presidents of our country.

"Hello, it's a pleasure to meet you." The homeowner approached Dad, extending a hand. Naturally, Dad pulled him into a hug, giving him a pat on the back.

"It's an honor to meet you, Mr. President." Dad, emotional, stepped back.

"Oh, I haven't been president for a few years now." Arnold gave an embarrassed smile.

"In the hearts of Americans, you always will be," Dad said, as always, moved by his words.

If he didn't do that, it wouldn't be him.

"Can we sit and talk? Zachary is at the Capitol, but he'll be here soon. There was an emergency meeting, and he apologized; he'll come as quickly as possible." Arnold tried to smile, clearly giving a forced grin.

"Just because I admire you doesn't mean I'll like your son; that's one point against him," Dad grumbled, irritated.

Great, did we really need that meeting?

CHAPTER TWENTY-SEVEN

Zachary

That meeting wasn't supposed to happen; I wasn't supposed to be here. William decided to structure a new set of laws that ended up taking more of our time. I kept checking my watch to see the time. The Bellinghams had already arrived at my parents' house; I knew that from the message Dad sent me.

When all the clauses were finally decided, we concluded the meeting, and I quickly got up from my chair.

"In such a hurry, Zach," my cousin said nonchalantly.

"Did you forget I have an appointment at my parents' house today?" I asked, speaking in a way that the others wouldn't understand what I meant, revealing only the word 'appointment,' so William would know what I was talking about.

"Why didn't you say so earlier?" He crossed his arms and squinted at me.

"There was no need; my work always comes first." I shrugged and turned my back.

With just a brief wave of goodbye, I left the meeting room and, putting on my jacket, hurried down the corridors of the Capitol.

MY DRIVER PARKED IN front of my parents' house. The lights were all on, and next to it, that enormous RAM truck was just what I expected—a monstrous pickup compared to what his daughter had. Mr. Peter Bellingham didn't even accept one of our private jets to come faster.

I hurriedly walked up the few steps. I opened the door myself, without waiting for Mary to do it—there was no need. I was more than half an hour late, and without bothering to take off my jacket, I entered the living room, seeing the Bellinghams there.

I quickly scanned the room and saw the burly man in a plaid shirt—not a flashy plaid, but a neutral tone. The worn jeans and boots revealed what I had already expected from Savannah's father.

Sadie was on her grandmother's lap, Savannah's mother, who was wearing a floral dress similar to those the little girl used to wear, and a small boot on her feet, just like my girl usually did.

I turned my gaze to Savannah, who had that sparkle in her eyes, making me think we should put on a show. What would a man in love do in such a situation?

"Good evening, everyone." My voice came out assertive. "I apologize for my delay; I had to attend a meeting, and soon I'll need to travel again. William is taking the opportunity to get everything in order."

I continued speaking as I walked toward my future wife. If it was time to perform, I would make the most of the situation. I stopped in front of Savannah, held her chin, and her blue eyes widened as she looked at me. I noticed that tonight she was wearing sandals instead of boots, and it was nice to see her looking different.

I bent down, and Savannah didn't turn her face because I kept it forward. My lips lightly touched hers in a peck that, God, I never wanted to pull away from. They were still as soft and velvety as they were two years ago, tasting like paradise.

If paradise had a flavor, it would definitely be the blend of the lips of the girl from Arizona.

"You look beautiful, Savannah." My eyes met hers, and I saw the exact moment her face turned red, slowly lowering it as she tried to hide her blush.

I straightened up and turned to what would be my future father-in-law. Peter got up from the sofa, and I extended my hand to him, which he accepted but then used to pull me into a half-embrace, giving me a pat on the back. I did the same, but obviously gave a lighter pat.

"It's a pleasure to meet you in person, Mr. Bellingham," I said as we pulled away.

"Please, just Peter." He looked me up and down as if assessing whether I was worthy of his daughter. "I saw you as a kid on TV with your father."

"I feel at a disadvantage." I moved closer to his wife, who had stood up and put my daughter on the floor.

She looked very much like Savannah. Now I knew where my girl got her beauty from.

"Mrs. Brenda." We exchanged a kiss on the cheek.

"You're much taller than I expected." The good thing about them was that they didn't stick to formalities and spoke more informally.

"TVs can be deceiving," I said, bending down to be at Sadie's level, who was on the floor looking at all of us. "Hello, little one."

It was impossible not to smile. How I missed her! My daughter gave me one of her lovely mischievous smiles, taking two little steps towards me, standing between my legs. I held her around the waist and lifted her onto my lap.

After being next to her the first time, it was easier the second.

"Did you have a good trip?" I asked Savannah's parents without letting go of my daughter, moving to where Sadie's mother was sitting and taking a seat next to her.

"Yes, we did," Peter replied, turning his serious gaze back to me. "I don't like going around curves, so I'll get straight to the point: how did you meet?"

Great, the interrogation would be right off the bat.

"Dad, but I already told you on the phone..." Savannah grumbled beside me.

"I want to see if the stories match up, and I want to see how he will tell it." Mr. Peter kept his gaze fixed on me.

"We met almost three years ago, specifically about two years and eight months. I was heading to the Capitol when a girl with headphones, looking like she was in another world, crossed in front of my car. I was worried about her because she had fallen and could have hurt herself, so I decided to get out of the car and give her first aid. I took her into my car; she refused at first, saying she didn't get into cars with strangers, but after much insistence, she got in. I should have taken her to an emergency room, but since it was just a scrape, I figured I could fix it in my apartment, so I took her there. I think what fascinated me the most about her was that she didn't know who I was, she wasn't impressed when I mentioned my last name, except for asking for a photo to show her father." I smiled sincerely at Savannah, who was now looking at me with her mouth agape. "With all due respect, I think I was captivated by your daughter from the very first moment I laid eyes on her, but I sent her away thinking I wasn't worthy of such a sweet and beautiful woman. I could have gone after her when my engagement ended, but in my mind, she would be living a peaceful life, with *The Corrs* as the soundtrack. On the day of the accident, I noticed that she was playing that band's music on her phone. I couldn't bring her into my chaotic life."

I spoke all of this without dragging it out, hearing my mother's emotional sigh since this was the first time they were hearing how I met Savannah.

"And what made you change your mind now?" Peter asked. "I know Sadie plays a significant role in this decision, but a child shouldn't be the only reason for a marriage..."

"It's not just because of Sadie, of course, she was an essential part," I cut off Mr. Peter, having the answer on the tip of my tongue. "I realized that it took me almost three years to understand that I could have her by my side. I can bring *The Corrs* soundtracks into my routine. I want your daughter, Peter. I want the spontaneous smiles and the joy she can bring into my life. It's not just for Sadie; it's for both of them. I don't want to miss a single day away from them anymore."

It was easy to speak when it came to Savannah; she was everything I never imagined having in my life—sweet, beautiful, and loving.

I didn't look away, knowing that the man wanted me to keep my gaze on him. Peter scrutinized me for a long few seconds before getting up from the sofa.

"It was easier than I thought. I felt the truth in every word you said." I stood up from the sofa, leaving Sadie sitting next to her mother, and extended my hand to Peter.

He hugged me tightly, as if accepting me into his family.

"I approve of your marriage, but I want a real wedding. My daughter deserves everything—a church, all our family members..."

"That won't be a problem, as I'm already looking into a wedding planner." Mom clapped her hands excitedly.

"But before that, I want to make something official." I stepped away from Peter, pulling a velvet box from the pocket of my jacket.

I walked over to my future wife, easily kneeling in front of her and opening the box.

Savannah didn't expect this. Her eyes widened again as she bit the corner of her lip, a gesture I realized she made to hold back tears.

"Will you marry me, my Arizona girl?"

CHAPTER TWENTY-EIGHT

Savannah

Having Zachary kneeling there in front of me was like living a childhood dream—a dream of having a handsome man asking me to marry him, wanting me to be his wife out of love, affection, and devotion. It would be perfect if it weren't just a man acting in a scene, as that marriage would never be real.

I bit my lip, trying to hold back the silly tears. They shouldn't be there, they shouldn't be part of this whole scene, but I couldn't stop one from rolling down my cheek.

He wanted my answer, and in that beautiful little box was a solitaire ring with a small blue stone—it was perfect. All I needed to say was the resounding:

"Yes." The word came from my trembling lips. I extended my hand to the senator, who took my fingers and slid the ring onto them. Zachary brought his lips to my finger, kissing over the ring, and then lifted his face.

Once again, his lips came towards mine, and God, I wanted that kiss. I wanted to feel his lips, the brief brush of his beard. But I ended up lowering my face as if feeling shy, allowing him to kiss my forehead, turning it into a gesture of affection and care.

I couldn't let myself be carried away by Zachary's little performance. I was still replaying in my mind how he had snubbed me. On our first date, the way he said I wasn't the type of woman to be with him. We weren't compatible, and I didn't even know how this marriage would work.

The senator returned to sit next to Sadie, picking up our daughter in his lap. It was incredible how, at the last meeting, he didn't even know how to hold her, and now he was treating her as if he had known her since birth.

Dad ended up liking the senator more than expected. Zachary was good at the art of lying; it was becoming increasingly typical.

My daughter eventually returned to my mother's arms, and I stayed there, sitting and talking with all the guests. The women talked about the wedding, Grace wanted a wedding of the year, with everything possible, and amid all that splendor, my mother got excited. Before I knew it, we already had a wedding date set, and due to the elections, they wanted to hold it in a month. It seemed like a crazy short amount of time to me, but I ended up just agreeing.

"DAUGHTER, WAKE UP..." I heard my mother calling me, leaning on my shoulder.

"What happened, Mom?" I quickly sat up in bed, running my hand through my hair. "Did someone die?"

"No, but almost, if your father doesn't decide to grab the gun from your truck and start shooting at all those people taking pictures in front of your aunt's house..."

"What?" I jumped out of bed, but Mom stopped me from going to the window by holding my wrist.

"Don't go there, there are too many people. We notified the Fitzgeralds, actually, they already knew. It seems that some employee leaked the information that the housekeeper had an affair and hid a child from the senator. It's a huge *scandal*." My mother made a face, and I widened my eyes.

"It wasn't supposed to be this way." I returned to the bed, sitting down and slumping my shoulders.

"Everything will be alright, my dear," Mom said in her soothing tone, as she always did when she wanted to soften a situation.

My daughter turned on the bed. Sadie sat up lazily, her little eyes still closed, when she called out to me:

"*Mommy?*" I turned, looking at her without being able to contain my smile. She was the reason I went after Zachary. For her, I followed my intuition to find her father, wanting my daughter to know she had a dad, but I didn't expect it to end up like this.

Last night's dinner ended up being a bit strange. Zachary said goodbye in a rather cold manner, with just a kiss on the top of my head. In front of my father, he acted like the loving man, but behind the scenes, he didn't even look me in the eyes.

"Go get changed, honey. Grace called to say that Zachary is coming with security to pick you two up." I looked back at Mom.

"What?" It felt like I hadn't woken up properly and was living in a dream.

"Go get changed, dear..." Mom simply asked. "Let me change our little girl."

I nodded, getting out of bed and first going to the bathroom, washing my face, waking up to reality, and tapping my cheeks twice to make sure I wasn't dreaming—or rather, having a nightmare.

After finishing in the bathroom, I went to my closet, put on a pair of jeans, my boots, and a black tank top. I tied my hair up in a bun and went back to see my daughter, noticing her suitcase already packed by my aunt, who even included the doughnuts and cookies Sadie liked.

"I don't know what I would do without you guys," I murmured to Mom as she finished dressing Sadie in a onesie and shorts, and finally put on her sandals.

"Dear, none of this is your fault or your future husband's. Some bitter person leaked the news to all the tabloids." My aunt came towards me, giving me a hug.

I accepted it, knowing that when I stepped out, I would witness the chaos.

"Come on, dear, the senator has arrived," Dad said a little louder from outside the door.

I picked up my daughter, and as I was leaving the room, I saw Zachary entering through the front door. He had an annoyed expression, wearing beige jeans, a black polo shirt, and shoes that made him look like a *handsome playboy*. For God's sake, the senator looked deliciously handsome and irritated with that look.

"When I find out who the hell leaked this, I swear I'll kill them," he growled, pushing his sunglasses up onto his head.

"I have to agree with you," Dad said.

"I'll take the two of you to my parents' house. Since it's a gated community, the paparazzi won't be able to reach them. You can come whenever you want," Zachary informed, and everyone nodded.

He came towards me, lifting his hand and brushing his thumb against my cheek, which made me briefly close my eyes. I could easily believe in that whole performance.

"I'll protect you two, okay?" Nodding my head was all I could do at that moment.

The senator took my daughter's bag from my mother and then picked up Sadie in his arms.

"Don't stop, don't pay attention to any of those vultures, just keep walking to the car that has the door open for us, alright?" Again, I nodded my head in agreement.

We said goodbye to my parents and my aunt, and left. When they talked about chaos, I didn't expect the amount of clicking noise coming our way as we left the house. Zachary held my hand, guiding me to the car while holding Sadie in his arm.

Many questions were thrown at me, and I didn't answer any of them. In fact, I was quite terrified by them, they were too many and too cruel, such as: "Is it true you hid a child from the senator?" "Is it true you were planning to trap him with a baby?" "Is it true you were a housekeeper and are lying about your daughter being the senator's?"

Luckily, we were soon safely inside that car.

CHAPTER TWENTY-NINE

Savannah

I turned my face to see Sadie clinging to her father's neck. My daughter was scared, so I sat closer to them, running my hand down the little one's back.

"My *sweetie*, Mommy is here," I whispered, watching her turn her face towards me. "It's over, it's all done..."

Blinking her eyes, she didn't say anything, clearly dazed.

"This is what I meant when I said you weren't suited to be mine. I didn't mean you weren't a good person—you are good, Savannah, but not to be by my side, as if our worlds don't fit. The problem in all this is me. This was just a glimpse of my world. These photographers scared our daughter for nothing, and right now I want to punch every one of their damned faces." Zachary hugged our daughter as if he wanted to protect her from the entire world.

"If I'm not good enough to be by your side, then why are we having this wedding?" I asked, confused.

"We have a daughter, and this was the easiest solution to find..."

"No, Zachary, I won't accept you saying I'm not good enough." My voice came out determined and somewhat bitter.

"You don't understand. You're good, too good. You see no malice in anything, you have a good and light soul. My world is the opposite of that. What you know of me is my family, and we're all generous. I was raised by good parents. I know how to be like that, but I also know how to be treacherous. It's like a den of snakes, there are many two-faced people. They are kind in front of you but want to stab you in the back. I know this; I've been in a situation where a senator was my friend but was behind my back saying I was unfit to be where I was. That's what I'm trying to say. I want you to understand that we will be husband and wife, and you need to understand that there will be women who will pretend to be your friends and talk badly about you behind your back. There will be those who will desire your husband, who will say things about me to you just to make us fight, and the same will happen to me... My parents went through this; I lost count of how many times I saw Dad and Mom fighting when I was a kid over such issues. But they were stronger, and nothing broke their marriage. My world isn't at all rosy, but I'm selfish enough to let it slip from my life again." Zachary didn't take his eyes off mine.

I remained silent, absorbing what he had said, realizing that everything he mentioned was true. I wasn't a bad person, and everything he mentioned scared me, but I would be strong. Zachary thought he knew me, but I would prove otherwise.

"So, is that it? Do you think you know me? I might add a bit of dark dye to my rosy world." I shrugged, noticing that he cracked a small smile.

"You're impossible, Arizona girl. I hope I don't take away that beautiful essence that shines inside you." He lifted his hand to touch my cheek.

My daughter turned in her father's arms, moving from between his legs to our middle, staying between our legs, which I hadn't even noticed were so close.

"There's a doll in her bag. Can you get it?" I asked, and he moved to open the bag.

Zachary handed the doll to our daughter.

"You know, I wanted to have your phone number," he said as he gave the doll to Sadie, who hugged her little doll. That's what we called the doll, and everything I did with Sadie, she repeated with the doll.

"Your mother has it. I thought you'd get it from her." I looked up, meeting the senator's attentive eyes.

"I don't want to get my future wife's number from my mother," he grumbled, somewhat irritated.

"Remember that there's a caveat here, *future wife*," I murmured, rolling my eyes.

"Now more than ever, we need to make this feeling real. I've received millions of messages from Christopher saying that all our political allies are furious, and our rival party is sending jabs in the Washington D.C. Senate. I'm not one to do this kind of thing, but I need your help, Savannah. We can't lose our first presidential election. Christopher needs to win," Zachary seemed almost to be pleading.

"Well, I'll do everything in my power," I said firmly. "For me, you've already won this election."

I gave a small, sincere smile.

"Thank you, Arizona girl." He winked.

I noticed the car approaching Zachary's parents' condo and saw photographers there. The senator asked me to lower my face, and I did so, feeling his hand on my shoulders, protecting our daughter so she wouldn't notice the photographers.

When we passed through the condo gates, everything became calmer, and the chaos had passed.

"From the gate, you can see my parents' house," he said, and I deduced what he meant.

Our door was opened by Zachary's security. They were serious men, and only then did I realize they were armed. They weren't just drivers; they were armed security. That's why Zachary rarely walked around with Michael. He had more extensive security. It confused me, considering he was just a senator, though one of the most influential men in California. Hence the amount of security.

I walked around the car, seeing the senator's outstretched hand, and went to him, allowing him to hug me by the shoulder.

"How are we going to get out of these spotlight?" I grumbled.

"Simple, we need to make everyone think we love each other and that everything that happened was out of your fear, which is why you hid the pregnancy and our daughter. A statement has already been made, but I want you to read it before we release it, okay?" I lifted my face to meet his attentive eyes.

"Yes, that's fine, at least I think so." I forced a smile.

We entered the Fitzgerald residence, and Mrs. Grace immediately appeared, taking my daughter from Zach and heading to the living room with her.

"Grandma bought something for you; I'm sure we'll have a very enjoyable day." When I entered the room, I saw thousands of gift boxes.

"*Oh, heavens.*" was all that came out of my mouth.

"We need a distraction, dear. Come join us," Grace asked as Sadie jumped from her grandmother's lap, running to the many colorful gift packages.

"*Presents.*" Sadie clapped her hands, making us all forget the chaos outside and focus only on the innocent little girl.

CHAPTER THIRTY

Zachary

The anger consuming me made me want to interrogate every one of my mother's staff to find out who the hell spread that news. It shouldn't have been that way; Savannah wasn't meant to be exposed.

She came out looking like the biggest villain in the news. After all, it was Savannah who hid the child from her father. But I was also at fault; they couldn't dump everything on Savannah, not before she married me. She couldn't run away from me, couldn't have another bride running around. When, in reality, it was her I wanted, I desired Savannah with all my might.

I took my phone from my pocket, opened the messages, seeing a few from my cousins asking if my fiancée and daughter were okay at my mother's house. I replied to both, then opened Hanna's conversation, as we were still in touch, and her son was my godson.

Hanna saw the news and wanted to know how I was. I replied briefly, and of course, I answered about my daughter since I hadn't told her about Sadie yet. My friend made a bit of a fuss about me hiding my fatherhood from her.

I stopped in front of my father's office window, pushed the curtain aside, looking down, seeing something that displeased me greatly. Savannah was next to that driver; the way they maintained that friendship bothered me. I didn't like it, in fact, jealousy consumed me.

The driver ran his hand over Savannah's face, caressing her cheek. When he brought his face close to hers, Savannah lowered her face, just as she did with me, letting him kiss her forehead.

At that point, my blood was already boiling. I turned and ran out of the office, heading down the stairs two steps at a time. I quickly reached the back door, and they were still there, Savannah a step away from the man.

"Can I know what the hell is going on here?" I roared, clenching my fists.

My tone of voice made them both turn around, Savannah's eyes widening as they always did when something scared her.

"We're just talking," Savannah replied.

"Really? Because I saw him trying to kiss you on the lips when I was up there looking through the window," I snarled, moving toward the idiot who was my parents' driver.

"Cut it out, Zachary, of course not." I felt Savannah's hand on my wrist, trying to pull me back.

I pulled my hand away, knowing I wouldn't stop until I was in front of the driver. I wasn't going to hit him, but I was definitely going to scare him. Stopping in front of the man, my size was much larger than his. I grabbed his suit jacket with both hands.

"If my eyes see you trying to kiss my fiancée again, I'll forget that you're my father's driver and break your face. And another thing, keep your damn hands off Savannah. This isn't a request; it's an order." I pushed him back, releasing him.

"You don't have the right, Zachary. Michael is my friend." Savannah went to her friend, helping him to compose himself.

"A friend who can't keep his hands off you," I retorted angrily.

"He's been there for me when you weren't. Don't try to dictate my friendships when you have no power over me." Savannah came towards me, raising her hands, trying to push me, but I restrained her by holding her wrists.

"See this ring on your finger? It's a clear gesture that you're my fiancée, and what's mine doesn't get to exchange affection with another man. I hope that's clear." I pressed my face against hers.

Our noses were pressed against each other, our chests rising and falling with labored breaths.

Footsteps approached, but I didn't give myself the chance to look aside; I wasn't going to lose this confrontation.

"Can you two stop arguing? We can hear you from inside." It was my father, his hand on my shoulder, making me pull away from my fiancée.

"This argument isn't over. You're not going to dictate my friendships." She stomped her foot.

"When it's a male friend and he's touching your face, know that I will, indeed, do something about it!!!" I roared, watching her walk past me into the house.

I stayed there with my father, turning my face to the driver who was still standing in the same spot.

"I know he's important to her, and just because he was there for her when I wasn't, I'll spare his job. But know that I won't spare him again if I see him trying to kiss her on the lips. I'm not blind, I wasn't born yesterday. If Savannah hadn't lowered her face, he would have kissed her on the lips, and if that had happened, I would have definitely lost control." I was very explicit with my decision.

I didn't hear anything more, walked into the house, and saw my fiancée with my mother and Sadie, playing in the middle of the living room.

They had already had breakfast, and Savannah had approved the retraction note, which basically said everything, the truth with distorted words, making it seem like she started working at my parents' house to try to reconcile with me, where our love was rekindled, and we decided not to waste any more time, getting married and living passionately as a couple with her daughter.

In the end, love won. That's what was written. It hardly seemed like just moments ago we were almost killing each other.

"I want the wedding as soon as possible," I said, making my presence known.

"What?" Mom and Savannah asked, looking at me confused.

"I want to get married as soon as possible. I want you to be mine officially; I don't want this half-finished business anymore. I want to marry next week, like two crazy, passionate people. I know you can handle preparing a ceremony, Mom," I declared, exasperated.

"No! The plan is for a month..."

"We're not waiting a month. We're getting married next week." My voice was determined, though I was actually gnawed by fear that Savannah might decline, that she would find out how hectic my routine was.

I wasn't going to lose her, and that's why I wanted to move up the wedding, even if we had to go to Las Vegas to get married.

Savannah was going to be mine, and that was all that mattered!

CHAPTER THIRTY-ONE

Savannah

One week later...

It was the eve of my wedding. I should have been happy, but at that moment, all I wanted was to forget that social media existed, that my future husband was the most influential senator in the United States, and that his family seemed to rule over politics like a dynasty.

I sat on the bed, wearing the robe they made me put on after a day that had been amazing, the wedding day preparations. I had never been so pampered in my entire life.

The past week had been a whirlwind. Zachary had to travel to Washington D.C. and wouldn't be back until Saturday morning. I assumed he must be somewhere in that enormous house or in his penthouse.

Since our argument last week, we hadn't spoken, not by message or otherwise. How could I marry a man who didn't even bother to message me?

Well, it could be different if I sent a message, but I didn't want to give in. For that reason, I decided to wait for him to make the first move.

At least with Zachary away, living in the house had become easier. I had been terrified that he might argue with Michael, who, thank God, had decided to start a relationship with Olivia. They liked each other and were cute together.

Mitch tried to kiss me that day. It wasn't something Zachary had instigated, but I would never let another man kiss me while I was engaged, even if it was an arranged engagement. My friend misread the signals, thinking I was begging him to save me from the marriage when, in reality, I was just overwhelmed by the events of the day.

Michael apologized immediately afterward, saying he didn't know why he had done it since he was interested in Olivia. At least I didn't ruin their relationship, and they were still happy together.

In everyone's mind, my marriage to Zachary was real. Of course, the staff found it shocking and stopped me, wanting to know what happened. But the only person I briefly talked to about it was Olivia, who was one of the few staff members I talked to the most.

It was strange going from being a maid to one of the family members. They had already replaced me with another girl. Now I was the senator's fiancée; it seemed even holding a broom was forbidden.

It was easy to stay away from my phone that week, avoiding sensationalist news, but on the screen of my phone, with a photo of my husband and me side by side, there was an X over my face in a small photo. Next to it was Zachary in what looked like a coffee shop with a woman, Hanna Torpe, described as his ex-fiancée.

I shouldn't worry, after all, how fake was this marriage? He made a huge fuss when I was with Michael, but that only concerned me? Could the senator go out with his ex-fiancées?

I remembered the date; it had been two days ago. I tried to recall what I had done that day. It was when they were making the final adjustments to my dress. I noticed Mrs. Grace seemed a bit off, asking if I had seen anything. Even Olivia wanted to talk to me about something, and I just said it was a very busy day and that we could talk later.

And now, if I accepted that marriage, I would come across as a gold digger who didn't care if her husband was out with his ex-fiancée. If they already treated me that way, if all the newspapers portrayed me as the woman who wanted to siphon off the senator's money, now there would be no doubt about it.

How could this marriage save the Fitzgeralds' election if everything about me was negative?

A tear rolled down my cheek. I knew it wasn't anything like what was portrayed. But it hurt that no one would let me explain, to hear my side of the story. Even the Fitzgeralds releasing that statement was like nothing had happened; no one cared. *To hell with the girl from Arizona,* how could those sites be so malicious?

I even had to make my Instagram private because I was getting so many followers, most of whom were sending attacks.

Zachary didn't even seem to make an effort to address the attacks. It was clear he only cared about his political career; I was just a means for him to be closer to our daughter.

Where did I fit in?

Why didn't he make a single post on his Instagram about our relationship? There was nothing, just political content.

Why did everything have to change for me, while everything stayed the same for him?

Zachary said we would have a talk, but that talk never happened. My fiancé simply disappeared, and he chose to be photographed with his ex-fiancée.

I brushed my cheek with my hand, got out of bed, and if I couldn't even access the internet without seeing my picture as the gold digger, I believed this wasn't the place for me.

I headed to the closet. I had been staying in a room that had been arranged for me, sleeping every night with Sadie. But according to Grace, I needed to rest today so I wouldn't have dark circles tomorrow. What no one expected was that I would be so agitated that I couldn't sleep, and I ended up using my phone to distract myself.

I took off the robe and then the pajamas. I had received so many clothes, all different from what I was used to, but I decided to put on jeans, a tank top, and my boots. I needed to get my daughter and go back to Arizona, where I knew no one would judge me.

I couldn't take it. I couldn't handle all that pressure. I remembered saying I would endure it, but without Zachary by my side, it was becoming difficult, especially since he didn't lift a finger to prove he loved me. What a strange way to have a fake marriage where only I had to change.

I put my phone in the pocket of my jeans and headed toward the door. Downstairs, I could hear my little one laughing. They were all there. How had Sadie not gone to sleep yet?

I descended one step at a time, my footsteps noticed. They were all there, including Scarlett, Zachary's sister, who had arrived that morning. But what upset me the most was seeing Zachary's ex-fiancée there with them, with her child present, playing with my daughter.

"Savannah?" Zachary got up from the couch.

At that moment, anger blinded my eyes, and sadness overwhelmed my body.

"You said that your environment would make me give up on this marriage, but instead, you made me give up on it!!! I want my daughter, I want to go home." I headed towards Sadie. "TO HELL WITH YOUR ELECTION! I GAVE MY BEST TO BE THE WIFE OF THE SENATOR, BUT YOU DID NOTHING! *NOTHING*!"

I shouted at him, furious, out of control, and bitter.

CHAPTER THIRTY-TWO

Zachary

Mom said Savannah had gone to bed because she needed to be relaxed for the next day. She wanted to take our daughter with her but ended up leaving her with Grace after my mother insisted so much.

My friend Hanna wasn't having a good time. We met two days ago, and she said she was in the process of separating. I couldn't leave her alone, so I brought her with me to my wedding. I just didn't expect all that lack of control from my wife.

"Enough, Savannah." I pulled the girl into my arms. "No one is leaving this house, and our daughter is not going anywhere!"

I roared authoritatively, meeting her blue eyes, reddened with tears.

"Nothing has changed! You keep lying to me." She tried to push me but couldn't, tightening her grip on my jacket.

"I'm lying? When did I lie? I don't remember." I widened my eyes in confusion.

"Let me go so I can throw it right in your face." As I tried to pull away, she yanked her hand but didn't run; she just grabbed her phone, unlocking it and opening a page, holding it right in front of my face. "Look at the damn picture of my face! I tried, I really tried not to look at any damn news, but the first time I open my internet, a notification pops up!!!"

"That doesn't mean anything. Hanna is just my friend," I ignored the damn news and the picture of my future wife with an X over it.

"Just like Michael is just my friend, and you made a whole circus out of it last week. But that's not the point, it's not, because I'm not famous. The fact that I have a male friend doesn't make headlines, and my friend isn't my ex-fiancé." Savannah took a step back, tears streaming noisily down her face. "With me, during this week, there hasn't been a single photo of us together..."

"That's because I needed to travel. You know I'm going to need to travel several times..."

"Don't cut me off, damn it!!! There are no photos of us, nothing, just the two of us fleeing from my aunt's house. I'm fed up, exhausted! I have to pretend to be the passionate woman for everyone, while my life is changing. How do you expect everyone to think we're in love if I stayed here, you're in Washington D.C., and you didn't even post a damn thing on your Instagram? I know your politics are more important, but it wouldn't hurt to pretend once in a while. We know you know how to do that." Savannah wiped under her eyes. "I'm the one being attacked, and you're doing nothing to fix it... nothing..."

Her loud sniffle felt like something inside me was breaking. Savannah was distraught, and rightfully so; she had reached this state because I was fixated on my world, not even noticing how much she was overburdened.

I had focused so much on politics that I forgot to look after her. Maybe in a marriage, my career couldn't always come first.

"I want to leave, just let me go. I can't... I'm not a gold digger, I wasn't raised to be one..." The way she cried was one of pain and anguish.

I turned my face to my mother, who was also crying at Savannah's pain, a silent and calm cry.

"Mom, stay with Sadie," I asked, going to Savannah. "Come on, let's go upstairs. You're not leaving..."

"Don't touch me. I hate you, Senator, I hate you," she said, luckily already too weak to argue or run away from me.

I easily picked up the little one in my arms, walking toward the stairs. I didn't remember which room she was staying in, so I took her to mine. Savannah clung tightly to my jacket. I entered my room, going to my bed, where I gently sat Savannah down. She was supposed to lie down, but being as stubborn as she was, she remained sitting.

"I know I said I was strong and that I could handle it, but I can't. I don't know how long this fake marriage of ours will last, what its terms are. Even if we are married, can you still see other women? Including your ex-fiancé?" She started speaking, making me remember we hadn't discussed this topic.

"Hanna is my friend; there is no relationship between us..."

"How can you be friends with your ex-fiancé? The woman you were once in love with? I can't wrap my head around it."

"It's because I never had a real relationship with her. Well, not a real one. I was going to marry Hanna so she wouldn't be talked about poorly due to the pregnancy. It was the right decision. She was a good person, calm, and understood me. We would have had a good relationship," I told Savannah the truth.

"So you're saying that when we had that night together, you were going to marry your friend? A fake marriage like ours?" She widened her eyes.

"Not exactly like ours. Hanna is my friend; it's years of friendship..."

"Oh, right, now you're going to throw it in my face that we aren't friends," she cut me off, grumbling.

"No, Savannah, I wasn't going to say that. I was going to say that I don't desire Hanna. She's always been just a friend, as if we saw each other as siblings. But with you, it's different. I want you, I desire to be by your side, I crave every part of your body. And I only didn't come after you when my marriage was broken because I thought it was right to keep you away from me. You'd have a much better life without my interference."

I tried to be as explicit as possible with her.

"It doesn't seem like it. Not at all." Savannah pouted. "You left me here and went to Washington D.C. You didn't give any explanation, didn't say goodbye, left angry, not even a damn message!"

"I still don't have your number." I shrugged.

Savannah let out a long breath, grabbing her phone, unlocking it, and handing it to me.

"Write down your damn number so I can send a message!" Even when she was trying to make a drama, she was beautiful.

The Savannah in front of me at that moment was the dramatic one, not the one who had been desolate before.

I wrote down my number, handing the phone back to her. She opened her messaging app, sending something that vibrated in my pocket.

"Problem solved." She looked up at me.

"This problem is solved, but what about the other one?" I asked, raising an eyebrow.

"I need to know the limits of this marriage." Savannah wanted to know something I also wanted.

CHAPTER THIRTY-THREE

Savannah

Zachary stared at me for what felt like an eternity, as if we were waiting for each other to speak. Finally, he took the first step.

"Savannah, since you came back into my life, I haven't been with any other women. My thoughts wouldn't allow it, thinking of you all the time. But I am a sexually active man," he said, making it clear that what he meant was, either have sex with me, or I'll find someone else.

"So you're saying we'll have a... how should I put it... open marriage?" I cleared my throat, searching for the right words.

"It's more or less like that," he said. I nodded as if I was processing this fact. "Or we could have a real marriage..."

My head movement stopped, my eyes locking with his.

"That's out of the question," I said, shaking my head again.

"Damn, was it that bad that you don't want to be in my bed anymore?" he asked, sounding somewhat astonished by my refusal.

"On the contrary, it was good, and I'd rather not give in to a man who turned my first time into a disaster. I really don't know what's going on in your head. Here in front of me, you say beautiful things, sentences that could make any woman fall in love, but in front of others, you turn into someone else, a cold man with no displays of affection, as if nothing else mattered," I said, letting out what I'd been holding inside. "Fortunately, I know you well, Senator. I know deep down you're not committed to anything but your career. That's my biggest fear in this marriage—the lack of your commitment."

He fell silent again, apparently I was one of the first people to confront him with some truths.

"Is that how you see me?" he finally asked.

"That's how I see you," I said firmly.

"And you're right. I've never been in a relationship before. Well, actually, I was in one with a woman I truly loved, and my career was too much for her. I had to choose between her and what I loved doing most..."

"We both know the answer without needing to say it—you chose your career," I interjected.

"Yes, Lucy left me, and since then I promised myself I would never fall in love again. That's why I wanted a marriage with Hanna—we'd be friends and never involve intimate feelings."

"That's nonsense, one of the biggest I've ever heard," I said, rolling my eyes. "When it comes to love, there's no mind that stays sober to a passionate heart."

"You're like Lucy. When I almost ran you over, I thought you were similar—naive, sweet, and loving. But spending more time with you made me realize you're quite different. You are sweet and loving, but you're full of life, talkative, and don't hold back your feelings. You're the kind of woman every man would like to have by his side, even me. I was very afraid of ruining you, afraid my world would spoil you, and it seemed like that was happening right before my eyes and I didn't see it," he said, raising his hand and tucking my hair behind my ear. "I'm sorry. Maybe I don't know how to be in a relationship. I disconnected from everything when I was in Washington D.C., and that was my biggest mistake."

I closed my eyes, feeling Zachary's finger trace along my cheek.

"I don't know, I don't know if we should get married. I'm not sure if it's the right choice," I murmured, opening my eyes to find his face close to mine.

"And if I promise total exclusivity to you?" I noticed a hint of desperation in his voice.

"I thought you were a sexually active man," I said, curling my lip.

"Well, I am, but I'll be patient and wait for you."

"And what if I never give in?"

"It seems like I'll never have sex for the rest of my life," Zachary said, frowning in a funny way.

"I'm not sure I believe that," I whispered, thoughtful.

"Savannah, just don't leave me, don't cancel our wedding. I've never wanted anyone in my life as much as I want you and our little one. I'll try my best to be a good husband, but don't cancel our wedding... I'm begging you," Zachary pleaded. Was he really begging me, the senator, to not cancel our wedding?

"Beg a little more, and maybe I'll reconsider not canceling this wedding," I murmured, giving a sly little smile.

"Savannah Bellingham, my future Mrs. Fitzgerald, let me change your last name, be mine. I promise to be the best for you, to not put us in situations like this. If necessary, I'll have my staff post daily about how grateful I am to have you in my life. Just accept me as your husband..."

"Say the magic word?" I asked, biting the corner of my lip, enjoying the moment.

"I beg you?" Zachary raised an eyebrow, confused.

"Is the exclusivity part still on the table?" I asked.

"Yes, but it has to apply to you as well. I'm fine with going without sex, but I won't accept another man touching what's mine," the possessiveness was clear in his voice.

"That's not a problem for me. Once you become a mother, it's not easy to find time for men," I shrugged.

"So you don't usually go out with men?" The senator seemed curious.

"No," I said, looking around trying to recognize the room.

"I like that," he said. I rolled my eyes at his words. "Now tell me, can I expect you at the church altar tomorrow?"

I bit the corner of my lip, stretching out the suspense a little longer, and took a few seconds to respond.

"Yes, I suppose so..."

"Savannah." My name came out in a reprimanding tone, making me laugh, throwing myself backward onto the bed.

"Yes, Senator Fitzgerald, you can wait for me." I widened my eyes when I saw him place a foot beside mine, covering my body with his, but without touching it.

"I love the sound of your laugh, my Arizona girl," he said, looking down at me, leaving me stunned by his beauty.

"I need to go to my room; after all, I need to sleep," I quickly changed the subject.

"Sleep here with me," he said naturally. "Let me tuck you in..."

"I thought I had been quite explicit..."

"Savannah, no sex, just let me put my fiancée to sleep." Zachary got up from the bed, pulling the covers down.

"But I need to change clothes; I don't sleep in jeans."

"Go to your room and change, or better yet, use one of my shirts." He pointed to his closet.

That offer was tempting—staying there next to him, smelling his scent all night made the spot between my legs tingle with the thought.

"Alright." I jumped off the bed, seeing his eyes sparkle. "I'll go to my room, sleep alone. A bride shouldn't be close to the groom the day before the wedding, you know, it's bad luck..."

My sentence died when I reached the door. I bit the corner of my lip as I saw the sparkle in Zachary's eyes fade.

"You're still sleeping in my bed, Savannah Fitzgerald," he called me by his last name.

"We'll see about that, Senator..."

"I don't give up easily," he replied.

Before I could falter in my words, I opened the door and nearly ran out, breathless, knowing I was very close to giving in to him.

CHAPTER THIRTY-FOUR

Savannah

"Are you ready to become the next Fitzgerald?" My sister jumped on the bed, startling me awake.

"Hazel," I grumbled, pulling the covers, wanting to go back to sleep.

I had taken so long to fall asleep the night before that now I didn't want to get out of bed.

"You'd better get up, little sister, it's your day." Hazel pulled at my covers.

"Remind me to do the same when it's your wedding." I rubbed my eyes, lazily sitting up in bed.

"Oh, definitely. That day is probably a long way off." Hazel shrugged.

I looked around as if searching for someone, not quite sure what exactly it was.

"Where's my daughter?" I asked about Sadie.

"Downstairs with Mom. This house is a mess, so I came up here. By the way, I saw the senator's story, he slept here with you?"

"What?" I asked, confused.

"Didn't you know? Zachary didn't sleep with you?" My sister turned to look at me.

"No, I slept alone..."

My sentence trailed off as I saw my sister pick up her phone, coming towards me, turning the screen towards me. There was a *story* with dim lighting, it was the lamp light, and the photo showed me sleeping. I took the phone from my sister's hand.

Zachary took a picture of me sleeping?

And he even wrote in the *story*: **"You will always be my best choice."**

"Do you think he did this under pressure?" I asked, somewhat stunned. "Yesterday we had an argument. Actually, it was me who started it, because everything was falling on me while he showed no emotion, making the attacks never stop."

"Look, I don't know that man well, but he doesn't seem like someone who does things under pressure." My sister shrugged nonchalantly, turning back to the mirror.

I stared at that image for a long time, a silly smile forming on my lips. He said he would start showing his feelings publicly, and maybe he was already beginning to do so.

What we were doing was crazy. Sometimes it didn't seem like it was just for Sadie, but as if we both wanted it.

"ARE YOU FEELING BETTER, dear?" Mrs. Grace asked as I came down the stairs, wearing a loose dress, knowing that after having my breakfast, I would start getting ready.

"Yes, I am. I apologize for my outburst yesterday." I forced a smile.

"Dear, don't apologize. It was necessary. Zachary thinks nothing matters beyond his career, and it was clear from his look that he cared. My son was raised to follow in his father's footsteps, and when he lost a woman he loved, he believed that by shielding his heart, he wouldn't go through the same thing again. Zachary has strong feelings for you,

Savannah, and he distanced himself out of fear—fear of going through everything all over again."

"But he needs to understand that I'm not a mind reader, guessing what's going on in his head. He needs to know that I'm not emotionless, and that all those attacks online wouldn't affect me. How did he not see what was being done to me? In what parallel world does Zachary live?" I asked my future mother-in-law.

"You know, Savannah, of all the women who might have come into my son's life, I'm happy he chose you, that you two found each other. It's wrong of me to say this; I can't put the emotional burden of Zach on your shoulders, but I feel it from the bottom of my heart. You are the ideal woman, the one who will put my boy on the right path." Mrs. Grace's eyes filled with tears. "I'm grateful to have you in our lives."

Mrs. Grace opened her arms, and I accepted them. Hugging my future mother-in-law, I heard her sniffles and felt her fingers gripping my back tightly.

"Thank you, Savannah, thank you for being in our lives."

"Grace, please don't make me cry this early," I tried to joke, but my eyes were already filling with tears.

We pulled apart, hearing the sweetest giggle of my life, looking around for my little girl's golden hair.

"Mommy." My little one came toward me.

I bent down, picking her up into my arms. I hugged her small body, feeling her scent fill my nose.

"It's so hard to sleep away from this perfect little smell," I said, taking a deep sniff, dragging my nose along her neck, listening to Sadie's loud and delightful laughter.

STANDING IN FRONT OF that mirror, I looked at my reflection for a long time, barely recognizing myself in that long, strapless dress, with intricate beadwork on the top and a voluminous skirt with tulle underneath.

My hair was styled in a high bun, with wavy strands falling and my bangs pinned behind my ear, slightly falling on my forehead.

"I look beautiful," I murmured, admiring myself, with my mother right behind me and my sister on my other side.

Mrs. Grace wasn't there; she was arriving earlier at the church to make the entrance with Zachary.

That day, all I did was stay away from my phone, not wanting any bad news, nothing that would make me second-guess my decision to go through with this madness.

The door to the room opened, and in walked my father, holding my daughter's hand. They hadn't let me see her before, to make a surprise for me.

"Oh my God." I put my hands over my mouth. "She looks beautiful, oh heavens, the most beautiful little princess I've ever seen..."

"Handkerchief," my sister interrupted, extending it to me.

I took it, placing it under my eyes, feeling tears threatening to fall.

"Princesses." Sadie clapped her hands excitedly.

My father picked up my daughter so I could see her, as the dress made it impossible for me to bend down.

"You're the second bride I've ever seen, my dear." I smiled widely. "You're just not the first because your mother will always be my first."

He winked at Mom; I loved how openly they showed their love for each other.

"It seems the moment has arrived." I sighed deeply, holding my daughter's little hand. "Looks like we're going to meet your daddy at the church."

"Daddy." She stretched the "i" sound, having easily picked up that new word from us calling Zachary her father.

"I can't believe it, it's official now, I'm losing one of my daughters," Dad said dramatically.

"Dad, you're not losing me, I'll always be your little girl." I smiled broadly. "Please don't make me cry, it's just a wedding..."

"It's the beginning of a new chapter, my dear, it's not just a wedding." My father took the wedding very seriously. "Now, let's go; my job is to escort the bride to the altar, and I do it with mastery. I need to remind that senator that I know how to use a gun if he ever hurts my daughter's heart..."

"Dad," I scolded him, but couldn't help laughing.

CHAPTER THIRTY-FIVE

Zachary

It wasn't the first time I had entered a church to get married, but it was definitely the first time I felt my hand sweating. When I had stood at that same altar, in that same church waiting for Hanna, I wasn't euphoric, I didn't wake up desperately wanting to change my future wife's last name. This time everything was different.

If Savannah backed out of this wedding, I would surely chase after her like a madman. Even though I didn't know how to publicly express my love for her, I knew clearly that she was the woman from Arizona I wanted.

I clasped my hands, feeling them sweat, my mother a few steps away, the church full of people, all my relatives present, many of whom I didn't even remember but knew they must be important since Mom had invited them.

A large number of people were Savannah's relatives. A plane and accommodations had been arranged so that everyone could have a pleasant stay, although some preferred to come by car.

The wedding march began to play, and my eyes quickly went to the door, which was slowly opening. It felt like everything at that moment was testing my patience.

But when I saw the woman in white emerging behind it, my body relaxed. Savannah appeared completely in my view, so perfect in that white dress. Beside her was her father, a tall man seemingly willing to do anything for his daughter. And I completely understood that feeling, as I would do the same for my little Sadie.

Their steps seemed so slow that it felt like an eternity had passed without my girl reaching my side. My impatience must have been obvious to everyone present.

Finally, they approached the altar, and I took two steps toward my bride, extending my hand to where Mr. Peter was holding Savannah's, before handing her over to me. Our eyes met.

"Know that if I find out you're not giving my daughter the attention she deserves, I'll leave Arizona just to put a bullet in you." I didn't doubt it; Mr. Peter apparently treated his daughters like precious gems.

"I promise to protect and care for your daughter for the rest of my life," I said resolutely.

We turned to face the priest as the wedding march ceased:

"Who gives this woman to this union?"

"Her father, Peter Bellingham," my soon-to-be father-in-law responded, placing Savannah's hand in mine. "Love my daughter as she deserves to be loved, Fitzgerald."

Mr. Peter stepped away from the altar, and my eyes met Savannah's. She, like me, was nervous.

I winked at my future wife, giving her a small smile, as we turned to face the priest, who began the ceremony.

It was almost impossible not to keep my eyes on my little bride. I had to hand her a handkerchief since I wouldn't be able to stop her tears. I tried to focus as much as possible on the priest's words, but soon I found myself distracted by Savannah, thinking about how soon she would be mine.

Finally, the most awaited moment arrived: our vows. I faced my little Arizona woman, holding both her hands, our eyes meeting.

"If anyone objects to this marriage, speak now, or forever hold your peace," the priest said, and the whole church fell silent. I swear if anyone had spoken up, I would have killed them. Since no one did, the priest continued. "Savannah, repeat after me:

"I, Savannah Bellingham, promise to love and respect Zachary Fitzgerald, in sickness and in health, in poverty or in wealth, until death do us part," she said clearly, her voice trembling as the microphone was close to her lips.

The priest brought the microphone to my mouth, making it clear that it was my turn.

"I, Zachary Fitzgerald, promise to love and respect Savannah Bellingham, in sickness and in health, in poverty or in wealth, until death do us part." I gave a small smile as I finished speaking.

"The rings may be brought forward," the priest authorized, and we both turned our faces to the door as it opened again.

My little one was there, radiant in a white dress similar to her mother's. Next to Sadie was my sister; they both looked perfect.

Scarlett wore a white dress, a beautiful bridesmaid's dress, but it was simpler and more delicate than Savannah's, so as not to overshadow the bride.

Sadie began to quicken her steps as she approached us, opening a smile that turned into a delightful laugh echoing throughout the church. I bent down as she came closer, my little one extending her hand holding a pillow with the two rings.

"Daddy loves you, my little one," I whispered, bringing my lips to her forehead and giving her a kiss.

Sadie wanted to stay with us, but ended up going with my sister.

I straightened up, facing Savannah. We exchanged our rings, the tears that had stopped began to fall from my bride's eyes again. I slipped the ring onto her ring finger, seeing how perfectly it suited her. Savannah did the same, and I smiled seeing her fingers trembling as they held mine.

After we finished exchanging rings, the priest said a few more words and then spoke the phrase I had eagerly awaited:

"I now pronounce you husband and wife; what God has joined together, let no man put asunder. The groom may kiss the bride." The guests rose from their seats.

I held my new wife's face in my hands, saying:

"Finally, my Mrs. Fitzgerald." I opened my smile and pressed my lips to hers.

I didn't want just a peck; I wanted more. I encouraged her lips to open, giving her a real kiss, feeling her shy tongue touch mine, not releasing her face.

"Mine, only mine," I whispered as our lips slowly parted.

"Mine, only mine," she murmured, opening one of her beautiful smiles.

At that moment, she could ask me for anything, and my answer would be a resounding yes...

CHAPTER THIRTY-SIX

Savannah

We got into the limousine, struggling due to the large number of photographers outside.

"Your mother even rented a limousine?" I declared in surprise.

"Mrs. Grace always thinks of every detail," Zachary replied beside me.

"I really wish our little girl were here with us," I declared, missing Sadie.

"She's safe with your parents. It would be too crazy for her to face those photographers; I didn't want her in the middle of all this chaos," Zachary responded as the car took us to the party location.

"Was it always this chaotic when you were a kid?" I asked curiously.

"Yes, I come from a long line of politicians—my great-grandfather, my grandfather, my father, and the predecessors I haven't mentioned." His hand held mine, his fingers caressing mine slowly. "When I was a kid, I didn't quite understand it. I always had security with me, just like Scar did and still does. She doesn't like it much, but we can't take any risks with the safety of any family member."

"So Sadie will also have security following her around?" I asked, somewhat alarmed.

"Yes, and you too."

"Me too? But why me?" I didn't expect to have security.

"Savannah, you're my wife. We're a family with significant assets; anyone might want to kidnap you just to get a high ransom, or even worse. I would never leave my wife vulnerable." With his other hand, he touched the corner of my cheek.

"When I think nothing else can surprise me, something more always comes along," I whispered, reflecting.

"My dear, it's not as difficult as it seems." I lifted my eyes to meet his gaze as he called me that. "You asked me to be a true husband in front of others. We can practice when we're alone."

He winked playfully.

"As long as these practices don't involve intimate contact." He rolled his eyes, and I smiled. "Oh, I thought your stories this morning were very cute."

"Did you?" His finger approached my lips; I quickly closed my eyes, then opened them again.

"Yes, I did," I declared when he touched the corner of my lip. "Do we need to talk about that kiss in the church?"

"I liked it; we could do it more often." The senator leaned his face closer to mine.

"You're breaking an agreement; I don't remember agreeing to kisses..." My sentence died when he tried to kiss me, and I turned my face.

"Savannah," he grumbled, sounding frustrated.

"Did someone say it would be easy, Senator Fitzgerald?" I looked at him again when he pulled away.

"The girl I met almost three years ago was a bit more pliable than this one," he murmured, touching my chin again.

"The girl from almost three years ago was young, a virgin, and still believed in fairy tale princes, that was until her prince turned into a frog," I said, making him twist his lip and causing me to laugh.

"Wow, I've been compared to many things in my life, but never a frog. Up until now, I was being called a prince, which gave me some pride, but a frog?"

"Zachary, let's be honest; no girl should lose her virginity and then hear she's not the type for the same man with whom she just had her first time." I was honest with my thoughts.

"And that's why I'm reaping all the consequences of not being able to have you completely." He sighed heavily as he finished speaking.

"You're right, Senator." I gave a brief, mischievous smile.

"I prefer you to call me Zach; I like how it sounds on your lips," he murmured, not taking his eyes off my mouth.

"Maybe I shouldn't do that anymore then; provoking your instincts isn't what I plan to do," I said, although Grace had instructed me to tease my husband.

When they said mothers-in-law were terrible, it definitely didn't apply to mine. Grace was a sweetheart, almost like a mother to me. Before she went to the church today, she said she had left many short robes and baby-dolls in my closet to provoke my husband. According to Grace, I needed to make Zachary work hard for what he wanted so that when he got it, he would truly value it.

"You provoke me just by smiling at me." Zachary touched my lip with his thumb.

"Zachary, we're not going to kiss..."

"Yes, I know... but that doesn't stop me from continuing to try until I get what I want." He winked playfully.

"You're very full of yourself, Senator." I turned my face, shaking my head, unable to hide the smile on my face.

In the end, I was happy with the marriage. I knew Zachary was a good man, but the things he had said to me in the past, the way he had acted when he saw me back at his mother's house, still lingered in my mind. It replayed something I feared might happen again, which is why I preferred to stay sober rather than give in to the desperate need to be in the senator's arms.

What woman could resist the charms of Zachary Fitzgerald? Yes, I would manage, I would be the first, or I would try until my last hope.

"Savannah?" Zachary called me, pulling me out of my reverie.

"Yes?" I asked, looking into his eyes again.

"Thank you for not giving up on our marriage. I understand that I made a mistake going to Washington D.C. without giving you any explanation. I promise it won't happen again." My eyes fixed on our joined hands, his long fingers over mine, how they fit together perfectly.

"I could say I never run from a commitment, but I admit that yesterday I really wanted to run from all of this." I lifted my head, forcing a smile for him.

"Were you really going to cancel our wedding?"

"Yes, I was..." I bit the corner of my lip under his evaluative gaze.

"Promise me that if I do something foolish, if I act irresponsibly with our marriage, you'll tell me? Alert me if I do something like that?" he asked seriously.

"Yes, I promise."

"Don't jump to conclusions without talking to me. I might not even realize what I'm doing. All of this is new to me, but if there's one thing I'm certain of, it's about our marriage. I want you, Savannah." Zachary, when he wanted to show confidence and sincerity in his words, didn't look away, which made me believe him.

"On this matter, I believe you, Senator." With a small smile, I lifted my hand to touch my husband's soft beard.

Zachary placed his hand over mine. Seeing him close his eyes briefly, but as the car slowed down, he opened them. I pulled my hand away, realizing we had arrived at the luxurious venue where our wedding reception would take place.

Why did I still get surprised by the Fitzgeralds?

CHAPTER THIRTY-SEVEN

Savannah

I managed to sneak away and sit in an armchair tucked away in a corner of the party hall. From there, I could see my sister dancing with Scarlett and another girl who had been introduced as the sister of one of the senators from Chicago. From what I gathered, the two were from California, and when their parents separated, the brother ran for office in that state while she stayed with their mother in Sacramento.

Zoey was a friend of Scarlett's, bringing the three girls together.

I let out a long sigh, feeling my toes throbbing.

Sadie had fallen asleep in my lap about an hour ago. My daughter had been placed in a nursery specially designed for children. Grace had even thought of her granddaughter, who might feel tired and want to rest.

I lifted my face as I saw a woman approaching. I recognized her as Hanna, Zachary's ex-fiancée. I knew she was at the party since she had greeted us when we entered the party hall.

"Hello," Hanna said, stopping beside me. "Decided to take a break?"

"My feet are killing me," I declared with a grumble.

"I can imagine. I was already envying your energy, running back and forth the whole time." Hanna flashed a big smile.

"I'm glad weddings are a once-in-a-lifetime event. I definitely don't have the energy for another ceremony like this," I said, not realizing that Zachary had approached and heard what I said.

"Are you thinking about another wedding at our wedding?" He frowned in a funny way, stopping next to his friend.

"I'm considering the option of never marrying again," I teased, shrugging.

"Should I be worried about that?" Zachary casually placed his hand on his friend's shoulder.

Was it common for them to act that way in front of me? I shouldn't, but I felt that knot forming in my throat as jealousy started to take over.

"So, what are you two doing here?" Zachary asked, turning his face toward Hanna. I didn't answer, understanding that the question wasn't directly for me.

"I saw Savannah here alone and came to chat," Hanna shrugged her shoulders.

Zachary turned his gaze back to me. It was clear that they only had a friendship, but the way he treated her with affection made me jealous.

"Savannah?" Zachary removed his hand from his friend's shoulders and came toward me, clearly concerned.

Out of the corner of my eye, I saw Hanna stepping away. Zachary took my hand, helping me to stand, and then sat down in the armchair, making me sit on his lap.

"I'm fine, just with sore feet. You can go back to your cousins," I said nonchalantly, turning my face, playing it up.

Zachary held my chin, and I looked back into his eyes with that gesture.

"Besides your feet, why do you have that pout on your lip?"

"I don't." I shrugged, keeping one hand over the other, refusing to hold onto him.

Zachary looked divinely handsome, with his hair a bit disheveled from all the roughhousing with the other men, his tie removed, and the jacket gone, with the top buttons of his shirt undone.

"Savannah?"

"What a bothersome habit of thinking I'm hiding something." I rolled my eyes.

"You're not jealous of Hanna, are you?" I shrugged, making it clear with my gesture that I was. "My dear, she's just a friend. Nothing ever happened between us, not even in the slightest."

"Just leave me alone while I process the fact that my husband has a stunning best friend who was his ex-fiancée and that they hang out together," I said, not taking my eyes off his.

"Savannah Fitzgerald, are you a jealous woman?" My husband was starting to mock the situation.

"You are too, so we're even," I shrugged nonchalantly.

"But your jealousy is modestly, well, *cute*." Zachary spread his hand along the side of my face. "My dear, did you forget the agreement we made last night?"

"Which one?" I asked, closing my eyes, feeling his delicious touch.

"I'm yours," he whispered near my ear, making my whole body shiver.

"Really?" I bit the corner of my lip, feeling his kisses on my neck, his beard brushing against my sensitive skin.

"Yes, and you are mine..."

"Yes, I am yours." I parted my lips, letting a sigh escape.

"I don't mean to kill the mood, but we're in public." I quickly opened my eyes at the voice of William, Zachary's governor cousin.

"Damn it, William." I heard Zachary complain as I was already standing up in my embarrassment.

Out of the corner of my eye, I saw Zoey approaching.

"Sav, aren't you going to toss the bouquet? Maybe I'll catch it," Zoey said, looking at the governor, who simply ignored her.

"Oh, I will. I think it's about time," I said, still returning to my normal state.

"Great." She clapped her hands and walked away.

"Is she your fiancée, William?" I asked, confused. I knew he had a fiancée, but I didn't realize it was Zoey.

"No, she's the one who wanted to be his fiancée," Zachary replied, getting up from the armchair.

"Zoey is crazy; she's lost all sense of sanity. Her brother is my best friend, and all her youthful spirit tires me just looking at it. Keith, my fiancée isn't here," William concluded, looking at me.

"They only see each other once a month, and there are always rumors that their engagement is a complete sham, all just for marketing," Zachary added.

"I don't care. Keith is fine, that's all," William shrugged and walked away.

"Does he really have a convenience fiancée?" I asked Zachary once we were alone.

"I've had one too, so I don't judge him. Just be careful with Zoey; she's a bit crazy, but in a good way. Just don't get swayed by her craziness." He shook his head as he accompanied me to the area where the bouquet toss was going to happen.

"It seems like she, Scarlett, and Hazel really hit it off." We approached the circle.

"Of course, they have something in common—the *craziness*," Zachary said, teasingly, giving me a quick kiss on the lips. "Just, please, don't throw that bouquet to Scar. I don't want to see my little sister getting married."

I nodded as the event coordinator, who had been assisting me all the time, handed me the bouquet.

I laughed watching all the single women organizing themselves. I turned around, not knowing their exact positions, counted to three with everyone, and tossed the bouquet. Zoey's joyful scream rang out.

I moved, seeing the girl with long black hair shaking her bouquet. Shamelessly, she turned and sought out William, holding the bouquet up for him to see from a distance.

"All you have to do is admit that it's by my side you want to be." Obviously, her crush wasn't a secret, as everyone laughed and William just ignored the poor girl, who seemed unfazed by his refusal.

CHAPTER THIRTY-EIGHT

Savannah

The car moved through the silent night, with our sleeping daughter in Zachary's lap. Sadie was in such a deep sleep that when we left the wedding, she merely murmured and went back to sleep.

Neither Zachary nor I said anything. It was to be our first night as a married couple, and I didn't know what to expect. Maybe I should hide in a room with Sadie. I had no idea what might happen.

The car entered the parking garage and parked in a spot. My door was opened, and I got out, holding onto the security guard's hand. I was still wearing that long dress, with only the tulle removed. According to my parents, the groom had to remove the dress, as it would bring more luck to our union.

I agreed out of fear of refusing and having them doubt the authenticity of our marriage.

I followed Zachary, who was carrying Sadie in his arms. We stopped in front of the elevator, and I pressed the top button. The doors quickly opened. We entered, and I looked up at Zachary, noticing that he was watching me.

"The last time I was here, my knee was in pretty bad shape," I said with a half-forced smile.

"The last time you were here, a girl was created," Zachary teased.

"Details that can be spared," I murmured, feeling my cheeks warm.

"I hope you haven't forgotten what your father said," Zachary's tone made it clear what he was referring to.

"I bet I can't take off your clothes," I said without thinking, aware that my face had turned several shades of red.

"Do you want to take off my clothes, wife?" There was much teasing in his voice.

"No, of course not," I said, inadvertently recalling that on our first meeting, he mentioned he wouldn't let any other woman touch him intimately. — Just then, the elevator doors opened.

I stopped in front of the penthouse entrance, waiting for him to appear and enter the code to let us in.

"1508," Zachary said in a clear tone for me to enter on the keypad.

I did so, remembering that date from somewhere, until it came to mind.

"Wait, that's the day we met." As I opened the door, I saw Zachary pass by me.

"The date I met the most charming girl," he said, heading toward one of the rooms.

As I followed him, I looked around, somewhat dazed, remembering that day I had been here. The memories of my first time came flooding back. Everything was the same, but it wasn't. Now, I wore a wedding dress, and a sweet little girl slept in the lap of the man who saved me.

Almost three years had passed, a time that completely changed our lives.

"Savannah?" I looked up, realizing I had stopped walking. "Sadie is asking for you."

"Oh, yes, I'm coming," I said, resuming my walk toward him.

Years could have passed, but I still remembered the path to his room. We entered, and I saw my little girl in the pajamas we had put on her at the reception. Sadie was rubbing her eyes.

"Mama," she mumbled, curling up again on the large bed.

"She just wanted to make sure she wasn't alone," I whispered, looking at Zachary, who had a puzzled frown. "She might recognize that you're her father, but I'm still the first person she looks for."

I shrugged, smiling confidently.

"I'm good at persuasion; I can change that," he said, coming toward me.

I looked around, searching for a place to escape.

"Savannah, you don't need to look so scared, I'm not going to do anything. I just want to take off your dress; I won't be the one to test the Bellingham superstitions." He gave a small, sideways smile.

"I don't know if I want to." Before I knew it, he was already behind me, unbuttoning the small buttons of my dress.

"In the closet, there are some clothes for you. I didn't have a room made for our daughter because this won't be our permanent residence in California. In fact, I'm thinking of either selling this penthouse or just leaving it to a family member."

"What? — I turned my face, looking at him over my shoulder.

"We're going to have a house of our own, one here in Sacramento near my parents, and one in Washington D.C. If Chris wins, we'll have to live there." His hand touched my shoulder, sliding the dress off my shoulders.

"So, does that mean we're going to live in Washington D.C.?" I asked.

"Yes."

"I've never been there," I murmured, "but Hazel talked to Natalie, and she plans to intern at their law firm, so I won't be alone."

"Does Christopher know about this?" I shrugged as my husband removed my dress.

"If he knows, I don't know. But Hazel really liked your aunt. Does your cousin not like my sister?"

"Actually, Chris is a bit of a grump. Anything that shows even a hint of joy makes him look like he's about to vomit," the way he spoke made me smile.

"I think we're done with the dress. Our wedding continues to follow the superstitions." I was left in a corset that squeezed my waist and a bra that kept my breasts covered.

"I didn't like this lingerie much; I was hoping for a clearer view." He pouted.

"Maybe next time, Senator," I said with a confident smile, stepping out of the pile of fabric on the floor.

I turned toward the door, knowing it led to the suite. I needed a mirror and a bit of privacy to remove all the pins from my hair.

"This view has made me a little happier." I placed both hands over my bottom, practically running toward the bathroom.

Obviously, Zachary let out one of his low, pleasant laughs that anyone would enjoy hearing.

CHAPTER THIRTY-NINE

Zachary

I felt something slide across my face, recognizing the small, delicate hand of my daughter.

"Daddy" Sadie's call was changing, perhaps because her voice was soft and a bit raspy, indicating that she had just woken up.

Slowly, I opened my eyes and glimpsed Sadie with her little face right on mine. It was impossible not to break into a big smile at the sight of that tiny perfection right beside me.

"Hello, my little one." I lifted my hand to touch my daughter's chubby cheeks.

"I woke up, mommy" just as she said daddy with an extra "n" at the end, she did the same with mommy.

"Did Daddy forget that now he has two women to wake him up?" My eyes caught Savannah sitting up on the bed, running her hand through her long blonde hair.

"Or would it be better to say one and a half?" I joked with a mix of affection. "Someone pinch me; I think I'm still dreaming."

I wished for Savannah and Sadie to be with me, as it was everything I wanted. If someone had asked me a month ago if I wanted a wife and children, I would have definitely refused. But just having Sadie, her being real, a little, beautiful, and adorable thing, mine and Savannah's, made everything different.

They changed all my concepts, all the goals I had set. I want them, I want Savannah and Sadie. I want them forever by my side.

"Do you really want to be pinched? Because I don't like being aggressive." Savannah made a face that made me smile.

"Let's save it for next time." I winked.

I sat up. Sadie held onto my shoulder, jumping on the bed, soon losing her balance and falling into the middle of us.

"I can go to your kitchen and prepare something for us to eat," Savannah said as I held both of Sadie's little hands to give her support for jumping.

"I don't think it will be necessary; whenever I'm home, Mary sends one of my mother's house staff over to prepare breakfast," I replied, smiling at Sadie.

"Is there anything I can do? Everything seems to have someone doing it for you." Savannah made me look at her.

"Welcome to my life," I declared, noticing that my wife wasn't pleased.

"I don't like feeling useless, and that's how I feel. Will I just be the senator's wife?" She shrugged her shoulders, making me thoughtful.

"You know, my sweet, my mother is part of the Sacramento Women's Club. They help many NGOs with charity balls and more. At first, it might seem like something superficial, but their work is beautiful. Talk to my mother; I'm sure she'll love having her daughter-in-law by her side. Mrs. Grace loves showing off her relatives." I noticed Savannah seemed reflective.

"I'm not sure if I can be like your mother, elegant and kind." Savannah's eyes soon became downcast.

"My sweet, you're good at everything. But I don't want you to change anything to fit into my world. I want you to remain the same. The girl from Arizona that I met..."

"I'll be crushed by this way of mine," she murmured, thoughtful.

"I'll never let that happen." I released one of Sadie's hands, reaching out to touch Savannah's chin, making her look at me.

"You said this would happen, that people would want to step on me. How can I deal with that?"

"If anyone does that, I'll take care of it myself. Savannah, there will be people who are malicious and will want to step on you, but I won't let them. Your sweet nature will be a point of envy for many." She nodded her head in agreement.

Sadie let out a little squeal, causing us both to shift our focus to her as she had the most beautiful smile on her face.

"What do you think about having our first family breakfast together?" Savannah transformed into the lioness of the family in seconds.

"Mommy always has the best ideas." I got up from the bed, casually rubbing my belly, noticing that Savannah had seen my gesture.

"Don't you have shirts in your closet?" she grumbled.

"I do, but I don't like sleeping in a shirt." I winked at my daughter. "Have you two already changed? Did you do that while I was sleeping?"

I furrowed my brow, realizing I had been tricked; neither of them was wearing pajamas anymore.

"Daddy has such a deep sleep..."

"Actually, I was dead tired. Luckily, weddings are a once-in-a-lifetime thing," I repeated her phrase with a mischievous smile.

"It's a good thing this bride didn't run off." Savannah reached out her hand to our daughter.

"I love your sense of humor, wife." I turned to head towards the suite when Savannah spoke, catching my attention.

"What is this boot doing here?" she asked, and I looked where she was pointing, at the boot in the corner of my furniture.

"The last time you were here, you left in such a rush that you forgot your boots." I shrugged as if Savannah had forgotten it the previous day.

"Zachary, that was almost three years ago." She looked at me with wide eyes.

"Are you sure? I thought it was just yesterday." I gave a half-smile.

"Why did you keep it? You could have just thrown it away." My eyes went back to our daughter, sitting in the middle of the bed, the little one playing with the sheets.

"To remind me every day of the wonderful woman I let slip away from my home, to never forget that I wasn't ruining her life when I brought her into mine." I let out a long sigh as I finished speaking.

"Even so, you brought me back..."

"Yes, I did. I couldn't bear the thought of letting you slip away a second time, knowing we have a daughter, and having to see you only as Sadie's mother, not as my girl. I decided to face all my fears, being selfish, bringing you back into my life, promising myself that I would protect you from all the evil that surrounds me. There may be bad things, but there are many good ones, and those are what I hold onto." I smiled at the end of my speech.

"So you kept my boot for almost three years, you kept my boot." A beautiful smile shone on her lips. "I admit, when I think I can't be surprised by my husband anymore, he comes along and shows that I still don't know him as well as I thought. It seems he's not so egocentric after all."

"Deep down, I'm the best husband there is," I joked, shaking my head.

"Conceited." Savannah grabbed a pillow and threw it at me. I dodged it, laughing, and went into the suite.

CHAPTER FORTY

Savannah

One week later...

The car pulled up in front of that luxurious house.

"Zachary, *but... but...*" My voice faltered as I stared at that stunning house, still somewhat dazed.

"Yes, I said it would be a small house, but Savannah, you deserve the best. I'm not going to give you less than I can provide." He winked.

The door was opened, and Zachary got out first. Since I was in the middle, he walked towards the other door where our daughter was beside me in her car seat.

I helped my husband unbuckle Sadie's car seat, a task he was still struggling with. I got out of the car and found myself lost in admiration of the residence. It was two stories high, with a high ceiling right at the house's entrance—or whatever you could call that entrance—with numerous windows revealing a spacious home with many rooms.

"Zach, how am I going to clean all this?" I asked, watching him set Sadie down on the ground. The little girl immediately ran towards the door.

"Who said you're going to clean? My sweet, we'll have the same number of staff as my mother. We have a housekeeper; she was recommended by Aunt Natalie."

"Oh, heavens, what will become of my days?" I murmured.

"Remember you said you didn't want to leave Sadie alone? Now you can spend more time with her. We can also hire a nanny for Sadie if needed. I know you're in touch with my Aunt Natalie about the women's club she's involved with here. Trust me, soon your routine will be full, and knowing the wife I married, I know you'll be involved in all the causes you can help with."

"Did you make a spreadsheet of my life? Because in the five days we spent apart, I didn't reveal anything about myself." I pouted.

We started walking when Sadie let out an excited squeal.

"I was checking with my mom." He shrugged.

We had spent five days apart, with Zachary wanting to come alone to get everything ready for my arrival and Sadie's. The house he bought was already fully furnished; he only needed to make a few final adjustments.

Even though we were apart, we talked every day via text. Unlike the last time he traveled, this time my husband was much more attentive, sending messages and wanting to know how my routine and our daughter were doing. We seemed like a real couple, with one exception: there was no affection or intimate contact.

Could we become friends in the end?

No, today when I saw him in that car waiting for us, my heart raced, my body tensed, the pain of missing him tightened in my chest. I still felt those same butterflies in my stomach when it came to Zachary Fitzgerald, but now I was seeing a different side of him—a more talkative and playful man.

We stopped in front of the door, and I held my daughter's little hand.

"Want to do the honors?" he asked, gesturing to the keypad where I had to enter the code.

"1508?" I inquired, wondering if it was the same code as the penthouse.

"Yes," Zach nodded.

I entered the code, the door unlocked, and holding onto the white wood—just like the exterior of the house—I pushed it open slowly. It was impossible not to look around in awe. The entry hall was breathtaking, high, with part of the second floor visible, from which a beautiful chandelier in golden tones hung.

In my other hand, I felt my senator's warm fingers intertwining with mine.

"Welcome to our home, my sweet Arizona girl."

"This is like stepping into a movie scene," I murmured in astonishment.

"This is what you deserve." I lifted my face, meeting Zachary's eyes fixed on me.

"You really are unbelievable, Zachary Fitzgerald." I smiled fondly.

"When it comes to my two girls, no luxury is too much," he said, and the way he said "my girls" made my heart melt a little. "Now, come on, I'll show you the house."

Zachary guided us to the living room. Again, I was amazed by everything. He continued showing me a tea room, a private lounge, the library, and in the backyard, an extensive yard with swings, slides, and even a playhouse for our daughter. In the corner of that same yard, there was a pool with a fence around it and a cover over it—safety was paramount with a small child in the house.

The kitchen was the place that enchanted me the most. Even though we would have cooks, it was there that I planned to make my homemade recipes with my daughter. There could be a million cooks, but nothing would take away my joy of spending time with Sadie.

Next to the kitchen, in another part of the dining room, with a huge table, was a bright and beautiful space.

"Wow, what a big table." I looked at my husband.

"I plan to have more children..."

"With whom?" I teased.

"Hope is the last thing to die, and in my case, it's far from dying." He winked confidently.

Zachary moved away, approaching Sadie, picking her up and asking me to follow him upstairs. We climbed the stairs, and I held onto the golden banister. The steps appeared to be light gray granite. Zach showed me several guest rooms, naming a few as the future rooms for our children.

Thinking about children made my world spin. Deep down, going through a planned pregnancy was what I wanted, to have a solid foundation, a husband, a daughter, a consolidated family.

"And here is my little princess's room." Zachary opened a door and set Sadie down on the floor.

Seeing the number of dolls, all the stuffed animals she loved, and the pink walls, Sadie ran off, enchanted by everything.

"Just a single bed?" I asked, looking at Zachary.

"Did you really think I would put a bed for you in our daughter's room?" He raised an eyebrow, looking smug.

"Didn't we agree not to sleep together?" I crossed my arms.

"Yes, we did, but until there are elections, we're sleeping together. We have staff, they'll be around the house, and what newlywed couple sleeps in separate rooms?"

"You used me, Zachary Fitzgerald, made me believe we'd be sleeping in separate rooms." I shook my head in refusal.

"It can't be that bad sleeping with me..."

"The problem is sleeping with you, and besides, Sadie isn't used to sleeping alone," I tried to find an excuse.

"We have a baby monitor, our room is right next door, we're away from the stairs, and if she wakes up, we'll hear her. Don't worry, my sweet." He winked at me.

"This wasn't in my plans," I grumbled.

"Well, plans can always be changed." His voice carried a hint of mischief.

CHAPTER FORTY-ONE

Savannah

My first night in the house was quite successful when Sadie asked me to join her in her bed. The little one just wanted me to tell her a story to fall asleep, so I told her the story and ended up falling asleep myself.

I stretched, realizing I had too much space, *wait*, this bed isn't Sadie's.

I quickly opened my eyes, realizing I was in another room. I turned my face and saw the bed next to me, empty but messy. Someone had slept there. The movement in the closet caught my attention, and out walked a man in a suit—it was my husband.

"What am I doing here?" I asked, somewhat dazed by the sight of that impeccable man.

"I said we'd be sleeping in the same bed. Don't pretend you weren't warned," he declared, adjusting his tie as if it needed aligning.

"But I thought I'd slept in our daughter's bed," I murmured, sitting up on the bed and running my hand through my hair, pushing it back.

"You did, but I brought you to our room, where you belong, next to me." He shrugged nonchalantly.

"How did I not feel you carrying me?" Zachary walked around the bed, stopping next to me.

"You didn't feel it, but I did. I felt it a lot. I must mention that you make some *very* sexy noises when you sleep—moans with your lips slightly parted, those soft sighs your little mouth makes, they drove me wild and made me want to wake you up right then and there," he finished, his face close to mine.

"That's a lie, I don't do that," I grumbled, biting the corner of my lip in nervousness.

"My sweet girl from Arizona, if my cock wasn't painfully eager to fuck you, I wouldn't believe it either. But I felt every muscle in my body craving to wake you up and lose myself between your legs," Zachary's hoarse voice almost made me beg him to have woken me up.

With a half-smile, my husband straightened up. My eyes traveled down his body, stopping right where his member was, seeing it outline the fabric of his dress pants.

"I have to ask, where are you going with all this elegance?" I asked, looking back up at him.

"I need to go to Christopher's house. We have some meetings with our party today and some campaign recordings," he answered, lowering his face to be right in front of mine. "Margo Lins, our housekeeper, is here. When you come downstairs, you can ask her any questions you have."

"Okay," I nodded, shaking my head.

"I'd love to stay here with you, but I can't..."

"Don't worry. Hazel is arriving today, she'll come straight here, and then we'll go to her new apartment. And there's Natalie; she messaged me yesterday wanting us to have coffee together. Until I really settle into a routine, I have a lot of little things to do," I said nonchalantly.

"And what about Sadie?" He wanted to know.

"She'll come with me. We have a stroller, and there's no reason to go out without our little one." I raised my hand, wanting to touch his beard, but Zachary pulled away.

"No, I don't want your touches. They remind me of something I can't have," he declared, rejecting my touch.

"Are you starting with this again?" I grumbled, rolling my eyes.

"Savannah, I'm beginning to consider the possibility of being touched by you, knowing all the triggers it could set off. Even knowing that I might give in and fall completely in love with you. But not yet..."

"But I touched your face; you let me." I pouted.

"Yes, I let you, and I enjoyed the sensation so much that I want to repeat it countless times. But, as with everything, there's a catch. You don't want to be touched by me, you don't want to be in my arms. When you give yourself completely, I might consider doing the same." His finger brushed my cheek.

"When you remove this situation of just 'considering,' I'll give myself completely." I shrugged nonchalantly.

"So you're saying you'll give yourself completely if I do the same?" He asked, raising an eyebrow mischievously.

"No more considering." I gave a brief smile.

"No more considering. I liked that." Zachary turned around as our door opened, and at that moment, our little one came through it.

Sadie dragged her little pink blanket along the floor, holding it in her tiny fingers.

"See, Mommy, how our girl can sleep alone and still come to our room when she wakes up?" Zachary's voice was filled with pride.

He went to our little one, bending down to pick her up in his arms. Sadie looked so beautiful in the arms of that suited man.

"Daddie." She raised her little hand, touching her father's face.

"This is what it's like to be in paradise—having a beautiful daughter and a wonderful wife." I felt my cheeks flush at his compliment.

My husband sat down beside me on the bed, placing Sadie on the mattress. She snuggled into my lap, opening one of her lovely smiles, curling up there.

"Now it's hard to leave and leave you both at home," the senator said, giving a small smile without taking his eyes off our daughter.

"I'm sorry to disappoint you, but you're going to miss some great company." I touched Sadie's little hair.

"Yes, throw it back in my face," he teased, getting up from the bed, leaning his face toward Sadie, and kissing her forehead.

He then came over to me, kissed my forehead as well, his large hands trailing through my hair.

"The proposal of giving yourself completely got me excited. I'll spend the whole day thinking about it," he winked and got up from the bed.

"You'll have good thoughts then, I presume." I watched him head toward the door.

"Oh, I almost forgot, tonight we have an event to attend. It's more of a social gathering. If you need anything, call my mom. She'll help you with what to wear." Zachary looked at me, curling his lip slightly.

"No cowgirl boots?" I asked, teasingly.

"I'm not sure if they'd fit the event..."

"Don't worry, husband. Your wife here is completely prepared for this kind of situation. Luckily, I have a mother-in-law who helped me with everything I needed to know during those five days we spent together. I even practiced wearing higher heels than I'm used to." I noticed a proud smile appear on Zachary's lips.

"You always surprise me."

With great effort, he left the room. I stayed there alone with my daughter, playing with her, dragging my feet to get ready and start a new day.

I asked Grace to teach me how to conduct myself in front of everyone who would be part of my husband's routine. I didn't want to seem *like a fish out of water*, so I learned many things, including how to dress, how to walk in higher heels, and how to avoid the women who only served to gossip about others.

I was more than ready for that event. At least that's what I thought.

CHAPTER FORTY-TWO

Savannah

My phone vibrated again; it was another message from Zachary. He wanted to know if everything was really set for me to go to that event with him.

"Are you and your husband talking at home?" My sister set the box down on the floor, looking at me while crossing her arms.

"Yes, we are. Why do you ask?" I furrowed my brow in confusion.

"You can't seem to tear yourself away from that phone." Hazel rolled her eyes.

"Tonight, I have the event with Zachary, and he wanted to know if I'm comfortable going with him..."

"And if you're not, is he going to skip it because of that?" Hazel always had a million questions, wanting to analyze every detail.

"I'm not sure, but I'm fine, feeling perfectly comfortable to face everything."

"Wow, what's going on with you, little sister?" Hazel made a face that made me smile broadly.

"I've just had a few lessons with Grace, and I'm loving all of it. You know, being able to wake up every day knowing I'm going to see Zachary, spending my day with Sadie by my side, taking her with me. Today, I met Margo Lins, the housekeeper. I have a housekeeper, did you know? This part will be a bit hard to get used to, but I want all of it. Strangely, I do. I'm happy, just like that." I patted my hand beside my body.

"Are you sure? Your sparkling eyes look like someone in love with the senator." Hazel had that suspicious look.

"Maybe I am, and maybe that's the only thing that scares me," I murmured, getting lost in my thoughts.

"It's clear from the way he treats you that there are feelings involved on the senator's part as well. But what worries me more is the fact that he doesn't acknowledge it and might end up hurting you like he did last time, letting you pull away because he doesn't think he's worthy of you."

"You know, I'm the one who should be giving you advice as the older sister." I gave a forced half-smile.

"Sav, let you gain some experience in relationships, then you can give me tips." Hazel winked.

"Oh God, your experiences can't be like mine." I curled my lip.

"If the Almighty up there wills it, they will be very hot, with some fiery men..."

"Hazel!" My sister burst into loud laughter.

"I'm glad I wasn't born with your puritanical spirit." Hazel turned away.

"I'm not puritanical. I told my husband that if he gives himself completely, I'll do the same." Hazel opened her mouth in surprise.

"Savannah Fitzgerald, you little minx. No restraints? What did he say?" My sister, who was about to grab the box from the floor, stopped, looking at me with curiosity.

"He said he liked the idea of us both being all in." I shrugged. "Zachary wants everything his way, and I know that sooner or later, I'll end up giving in. If I'm going to do it, it should be my way."

"That was a masterstroke. I want to see the senator get that out of his mind." Hazel went back to grab the box, heading to her new room. "Can you believe that the Fitzgeralds have such a beautiful apartment and no one lives in it?"

Hazel spoke a bit louder so I could hear.

"Sister, coming from that family, I don't doubt anything anymore..."

"A family that is now yours as well." Hazel turned back, clapping her hands on her jeans.

"Can you believe it? I love them all so much..."

"Savannah, your heart is too kind to hate anyone." My sister rolled her eyes.

"That's not true. I spent a long time hating my daughter's father."

"That's because you loved him too much." Hazel laughed again.

Just then, my daughter, who was in the living room of that beautiful apartment, let out a little scream, throwing her doll across the room. We both turned to see Sadie apparently having an argument with her doll, her rapid speech making it hard to understand everything.

"Oh, heavens," I murmured, torn between wanting to laugh and teaching my daughter not to throw things like that, trying to understand what made her act that way.

"That's right, my little niece, don't let the enemies walk all over you," my sister said beside me, and I turned to her.

"Hazel." I shook my head, going over to my little one, sitting beside her, playing a bit to keep her entertained while helping my sister with the move. My own move was already completed, thanks to my husband, who didn't want me to do anything.

Sometimes Zachary treated me like a delicate crystal.

"FINALLY." HAZEL THREW herself onto the couch. "Who said organizing a woman's wardrobe was easy?"

The apartment where Hazel was moving was furnished, but my sister had a lot of clothes, which took us quite a bit of time. She was the eclectic type, adapting to any environment.

"Luckily, this place has a huge closet," I grumbled, seeing Sadie asleep in the corner of the same couch.

"I've only got one thing to say: I'll have a good night's sleep with my lovely goddaughter, while you'll need to go out with your husband, Senator..."

"There's that, too." I closed my eyes.

"Luckily, you'll have my help getting dressed." Hazel jumped off the couch, her movement waking my daughter, who blinked several times, adjusting to her surroundings.

"I don't want to disappoint you, but she slept a lot this afternoon." I gave a forced half-smile.

"I'll make Sadie burn off plenty of energy, and by the time you know it, she'll be knocked out in her bed."

We started picking up things from the floor. I took my daughter in my arms and felt her little arms around my neck.

"My truck hasn't come yet," my sister said.

The truck that was once mine, I ended up giving to Hazel, since I had hardly any time to drive it now, and since it wasn't a double cab, I didn't like driving it around with Sadie.

"Zachary arranged for a driver for me," I said, seeing my sister flash one of her mischievous smiles. "Hazel Bellingham, stop looking at me like that."

"Okay, okay, it's just strange seeing this new version of you. Seriously, sister, it's doing you a lot of good. You have a different sparkle in your eyes."

"What do you think about us heading out soon? This talk about sparkle is quite odd." I curled my lip, ignoring the comment.

CHAPTER FORTY-THREE

Zachary

I rubbed one hand against the other, just like on our wedding day, feeling them sweat. Damn! Whenever it came to Savannah, I felt like a teenager.

"Daddy..." I lowered my face to see my little one extending her doll towards me.

"Do you want Daddy to put her to sleep?" I asked as Sadie began making baby crying sounds. "Oh, is she crying?"

Sadie nodded her head in agreement, so I began to rock the little doll in my arms.

"Music, music," my daughter said through her tears.

"Music calms her down?" My daughter confirmed authoritatively. "Have they told you that she's a bit of a temperamental one?"

I smiled and started to hum a lullaby, the first one that came to mind. Sadie clapped her hands when she saw I was doing it right.

"Only you could make me rock a doll and sing a song." I smiled at the lovely little girl standing on her toes, holding onto my knees.

The sound of heels on the stairs made me lift my face. I was so nervous that I quickly searched for my wife, and still holding the doll in my arm, I stood up from the couch with my daughter by my side.

Savannah was coming down first, with her sister right behind her. Obviously, my eyes were completely on my wife. The burgundy dress suited her skin tone perfectly. It stopped just above the knee and gracefully hugged all her curves. With only one strap, the other shoulder was fully exposed, and the neckline was discreet without revealing too much. Her long blonde hair looked smoother, flowing freely. On her feet, a higher heel than I was used to seeing her in.

When Savannah lifted her face, I caught a glimpse of the most beautiful woman I had ever had by my side. Her makeup was light, as delicate as she was.

My perfect wife.

I left the doll on the couch, took my daughter's little hand, and walked towards the two women descending the stairs.

"Wow... oh wow... you look stunning, Savannah," I said, somewhat dazed.

"Stunning, that's the word that perfectly describes you, little sister." Hazel whistled at her sister.

"Please stop, my face is getting hot." Savannah lowered her gaze.

"And your sister isn't lying; you'll outshine every woman at this event." I bent down to pick up Sadie, walking over to her mother.

"You're only saying that because..."

"Savannah, just accept the compliment," her sister interrupted. "My sister isn't used to this kind of praise, brother-in-law; you can keep it coming until she gets used to it."

Savannah rolled her eyes at Hazel.

"Sure thing." I winked in complicity with my sister-in-law.

"All I don't want is for you two to be plotting something." Savannah hugged our daughter. "Mommy is going out, my little peanut, but we'll be back soon. Be good to your aunt, okay?"

"It's not like we don't enjoy causing trouble together," Hazel teased. "Before you leave, I want to take a photo of the three of you to shut up a lot of people who said this was just for show..."

"Shut up," Sadie, who was in my lap at that moment, repeated what her aunt said.

"Hazel!" Savannah turned to her sister, who gave a forced smile.

"Sorry..."

"I like the idea of a photo." I reached inside my jacket, pulled out my phone, and handed it to my sister-in-law.

I held Sadie in my arm, placed my hand on my wife's waist, and pulled her close to me. I leaned my lips near Savannah's hair, knowing that doing so would make her give one of those sweet smiles and look up at me, even with her heels, she wasn't at my height.

Hazel managed to capture the moment and take the photo.

"Have you ever thought about being a model, brother-in-law?" Hazel said, coming towards me to return my phone.

"It wasn't on my life's ambitions." I took my phone as I spoke.

With one last hug for Sadie, I handed her over to my sister-in-law.

"Enjoy your night, say goodbye to Daddy and Mommy," Hazel said in a high-pitched voice, talking to my daughter.

We said our goodbyes and headed towards the exit, and before we left, I heard my sister-in-law shout:

"And make sure you give yourselves completely." I lowered my face, watching my wife blush.

"Let me guess, you told your sister?" I opened the door and watched her leave.

"We always confide in each other," she murmured, heading towards the car with the door open for us.

I sat in the back seat next to Savannah, her soft, sweet perfume overwhelming my senses. Everything about her made it hard for me to take my eyes off her radiance.

"So, does that mean you talked about giving yourselves completely?" I asked as the car began to move, shifting closer to her and feeling my leg brush against hers.

"Yes, we talked about it..."

"And what was the verdict?" I asked, curious.

"Well..." Savannah moistened her lips. "It depends on you now..."

"Do you want to touch me, Savannah?" I asked, not breaking eye contact with her, even though the car was dimly lit, I could see her face clearly.

"Yes, I do," she answered without hesitation.

"Then touch me," I whispered, tucking her hair behind her ear, bringing my face close to her neck, leaving kisses scattered on her skin, feeling her shiver.

"Zach," she whispered with a husky voice, I felt the tips of her fingers touch my hair, trailing down my neck.

"I love hearing my nickname from your lips," I murmured, sliding my lips over the lobe of her ear, hearing her sigh escape. "Control yourself; I don't want my security to hear my wife's sighs that are meant only for me..."

I whispered very softly, my lips brushing against her ear, making Savannah shiver again, and I gathered her hair into a ponytail with my hand.

Our eyes met when I pulled away.

"I want you completely, Savannah Fitzgerald, and I'm ready to give myself entirely to you," I murmured, my lips still grazing hers.

"Please, Zach, I'm almost surrendering right now." She closed her eyes, biting her lip. "My legs are weak, Senator..."

"Ah, my sweet girl from Arizona, how I wish I could fuck you right now, if this commitment weren't so important," my whisper came out with my voice breaking with the uncontrollable need to tear that dress off and have my girl right there.

But I had to restrain myself; I hadn't waited nearly three years for a rushed fuck in the car.

CHAPTER FORTY-FOUR

Savannah

The car stopped in front of the event. With the number of photographers there, I couldn't even distinguish what the place looked like.

"Are you ready?" Zachary asked before they opened our door.

"Yes, I am..." I didn't even finish my sentence when my door was opened.

I got out first, holding onto the security guard's hand, and then felt my husband's hand on my waist. Flashbulbs were going off in our direction.

"Just give them those beautiful smiles of yours," my husband said close to my ear. It seemed like he did it to provoke me, those whispers making me shiver as they touched my neck and ear.

Even though my legs felt a bit wobbly, I smiled at the lights, running my hands over my husband's back, feeling his tuxedo under my fingers as we walked on.

When he mentioned a small event, I didn't expect such a number of photographers. As we approached the entrance, they didn't even ask our names; they just opened the rope that was blocking the way.

"Why did you do that?" I asked once we were alone.

"Do what?" I looked up to see him playing dumb.

"You spoke close to my ear, you know that makes me shiver," I whispered, my eyes wide at the beauty of the ballroom as we entered.

"I wanted to get good pictures. Did you notice how the news about you is changing?" He made me frown.

"I don't know; I'm not looking anymore. What the eyes don't see, the heart doesn't feel. I'd rather think that everything I'm experiencing is perfect enough not to have that miserable crowd judging me." I shrugged as a waiter passed by with a tray of drinks.

"So, I'm perfect now? I went from a frog prince to perfect?" My husband gave me one of his mischievous smiles as we took two glasses of champagne and watched the man walk away.

"Senator, I never said perfection comes from you," I played hard to get.

"I will still be the reason for it." He winked, sliding his hand down my back and holding my fingers, making us walk hand in hand.

"Look, it's Christopher," I said when I saw Zachary's cousin approaching. He had a serious look, those piercing blue eyes greeting some people with a nod and stopping to shake hands with others. "Your cousin is very handsome..."

"You're calling my cousin handsome in front of me?" Zachary made me look at him and smile, clearly showing his jealousy.

"It's not like you didn't know, William is handsome too..."

"Great, now you're calling both my cousins handsome," he grumbled.

"Zach, stop cutting me off." I raised my hand to touch his face. "You're more handsome."

He tried not to smile but ended up showing a charming, self-assured grin. At that moment, Christopher stopped in front of us, and beside him was his assistant, the same one who was at Grace's house when they discovered Zachary's paternity.

"I see the marriage is paying off." Zachary's cousin gave me a quick kiss on the cheek.

"Who said it wouldn't?" Zach said with a mix of mockery.

Christopher just shook his head, looking around, but soon his gaze returned to me.

"Is it true that my mother asked your sister to come to Washington D.C. with you?" he asked, his eyebrows slightly furrowed.

"Yes, she's already settled into an apartment," I answered, noticing his look of disgust.

"I told him, but Chris didn't believe me; he thought I was bluffing," my husband shrugged.

"Nobody wants that sassy girl in our family's offices," Christopher's tone made me uncomfortable.

"You know, Christopher, she's my sister. I grew up with her. Besides being sisters, we're best friends. The one who doesn't deserve her presence here is you. Hazel is too good for someone as morbid as you..."

"Savannah," Zachary tried to get my attention, but soon began talking to his cousin, staying by my side, "but you deserved it, cousin. Hazel is my wife's sister, and whenever you speak of her, I ask for a bit of respect since only you hold that opinion about my sister-in-law."

Christopher fell silent, letting out a long sigh, and looked at me again.

"I apologize, Savannah. I was wrong to speak of her that way."

"You're forgiven, Christopher, but you know, right?" I held up two fingers and locked eyes with him. "I'm keeping an eye on you."

My gesture made both of them chuckle softly, as if trying to contain themselves in front of the other guests.

"You've found yourself quite a formidable wife, cousin," Christopher said amid his laughter.

"You have no idea how much," Zachary replied.

"Here comes our biggest target of the night..." Christopher's assistant made both of them straighten up and assume authoritative positions.

At that moment, I didn't even know what to think, so I just stayed silent next to my husband. A tall man in an all-black suit approached, his eyes fixed on Christopher, who immediately extended his hand to him.

"Christopher Fitzgerald, it's an honor to finally meet you." The two shook hands.

"Connor Backer," Chris simply said his name.

And at that moment, I recognized the surname; he was one of the most well-known hotel owners in the United States.

Connor turned to my husband.

"It seems the Fitzgeralds are always together." He extended his hand to my husband, who accepted it. "Zachary Fitzgerald."

"Connor," Zachary, unlike Christopher, only said the first name, immediately breaking into a smile.

"The last time I saw you, you were much more serious. You seem to be smiling a lot more now, Zachary." Connor appeared to be more familiar with my husband. "I believe I can guess the reason."

He said, looking at me as if studying me, and I felt Zachary's hand tense on my back.

"Pleasure to meet you, Savannah Fitzgerald." I extended my hand, not wanting to give any hint that I expected a kiss on the cheek.

"Already dropping your last name on her." Connor was a young man, possibly around the same age as my husband. "Connor Backer."

He shook my hand, and I quickly withdrew it. My husband pulled me closer to him as if marking his territory.

"So, you have a daughter. I thought those were just newspaper rumors," Connor continued.

"They're not rumors. I have a daughter," Zachary kept smiling, but with his hand tense on my back, I knew he wasn't feeling well inside.

"Can we talk about this another time, privately?" Christopher interjected.

"I know what you want to discuss. My father passed away, and he was one of your party's partners, one of its major supporters, I presume.

You want to know if I'll continue supporting you?" Connor looked at Christopher, who didn't smile.

"That's why I like you, always direct and to the point," my husband's cousin confirmed.

"Don't worry about that. You'll have my support in this election. If my father was loyal to the Fitzgeralds, you'll have my loyalty too." Connor raised his hand, resting it on Christopher's shoulder, which made Christopher look uncomfortable, though he remained calm out of politeness.

The men soon engaged in a conversation about politics, and since I understood very little about the topic, I remained silent, listening to everything they said, and at times, I even grasped what they were discussing.

Around me, many elegant women passed by, looking at the presidential candidate, but Christopher didn't seem to notice their presence, as if he was shut off in his own world.

CHAPTER FORTY-FIVE

Savannah

Zachary had been talking to many people throughout the hours, married men and their wives who asked me questions like how my daughter was doing—those were easy questions to answer.

Fortunately, we didn't have any situations that made me uncomfortable; in fact, everything was quite calm.

I felt Zach's fingers intertwine with mine as we walked alone to one of the corners, away from Christopher's presence.

"Where are we going?" I asked, curious.

"I need to get a bit affectionate with my wife; I can't keep smiling knowing I have the most beautiful woman by my side," he said softly, with his head close to mine.

"Here? At this event?" I questioned, confused.

"Yes, right here..."

His words were interrupted by a woman who stopped in front of us, clearly surprised to see the senator there.

"Lucy?" my husband said the name I had heard before. "What are you doing here?"

He asked as if seeing a mirage, his hand tightening around mine. The woman in front of me was very different from me—taller, with short, somewhat reddish hair, greenish eyes, and a lip gloss that gave her a delicate smile.

"Oh, my husband was invited to be here," she answered my husband's question, looking somewhat amazed to still be seeing him. "You know, Bernardo Lockeana is my husband..."

"No, I didn't know that. In fact, I haven't heard anything more about you," my husband said, moving his hand to my back, pulling me closer.

"Oh..." she cleared her throat. "You got married; I thought that day would never come..."

The situation was starting to make me extremely uncomfortable. Had these two had an affair before? Was I supposed to witness it all?

"Yes, I'm married. Savannah, this is Lucy. Lucy, this is my wife, Savannah." I politely extended my hand to Lucy, which she accepted in a handshake.

"It seems you found someone who finally likes your busy routine and is willing to run alongside you at all times," the way she spoke didn't sit well with me, as if she were saying a puppet was by Zachary's side.

"Actually, there's no need for running when there's love. My husband doesn't require me to go with him on every trip, especially since we have a daughter who will soon start school. We're married, not glued together. Every marriage should be built on a solid foundation of trust. I trust Zachary, and he trusts me. I know that if my husband needs to travel at the last minute, I don't necessarily have to rush after him, as we have our home where I can stay," I might have said too much, but I couldn't control my tongue.

My husband's hand caressed my back with more force, and Lucy in front of me opened her mouth slightly.

"Well, I need to find my husband." The woman, somewhat uncomfortable, turned and almost ran away.

I was alone with my husband again. I looked up, his eyes shining at me.

"Have I told you how perfect you are today?" he asked, using his other hand to caress my cheek.

"Did you know she was here?" I asked, avoiding the topic he had brought up.

"No, I didn't know. When I said I didn't know anything about her, I wasn't lying. Lucy is my past; you are my present and future." He smiled sideways, a small smile.

"So you don't feel anything for her anymore?"

"I haven't felt anything for a long time. When I didn't want to be touched, it was to spare me from feeling intensely what I felt for her; I didn't want to go through that pain again." He was honest with me.

"But now you'll let me touch you," I murmured, touching his jacket and giving a small, mischievous smile.

"That's because you've already touched my heart without much effort." He lowered his face, his lips brushing mine gently; my eyes closed. It wasn't a kiss, just a moment.

"Zachary, we're in front of everyone," I murmured, feeling my legs go weak.

"Sleep with me tonight, my sweet Arizona girl. Let me make love to you for an entire night?" he asked in a low, husky voice.

"Zachary... I... I..." I couldn't form a complete sentence.

"Just say yes, my love." I opened my eyes, meeting those intense blue eyes.

"Yes, I want to sleep with my husband tonight." I smiled with his lips still brushing mine.

"And what else?" he asked again, this time with a lot of malice in his voice.

"Make love until my body is tired." I raised my hand, touching his soft beard. "But let's not do it until dawn, my body can't handle it..."

I gave a big smile, watching him move away from me.

"I've waited so long for this moment that an entire night feels too short." He winked.

"You waited because you're a big *fool*. I've always been in the same place these almost three years; I never left Sacramento. So, theoretically, I've been by your side all this time," I declared.

"A big fool is the right description. I took too long to accept that I could have you, that you're stronger than I thought and can face any adversity around us..."

"Maybe what binds us is stronger than we think," I cut in, noticing Christopher approaching us.

"We can leave now; there's nothing more to do here. We've made all the alliances on our schedule, practiced good neighborliness. You're free to go, Zach." Chris placed a hand on his cousin's shoulder.

"Finally, I thought this night would never end," Zachary scoffed.

"You can accompany your wife. I'm proud to see you finally being a family man," Christopher teased.

"Now it's just you left..."

"I had my great love, and if God took her from me, it means I don't need another one."

"Or it means you might give yourself a new chance, Chris," I said, calling him by his nickname for the first time, smiling at him.

"Thank you, but I'll pass. I prefer solitude to having someone else by my side who isn't her," he said with a melancholic tone that even made me feel pity.

"That's a lost cause, my love." Zachary rolled his eyes at his cousin.

"Enjoy your marriage. Being married is good; just enjoy it," Christopher said.

We said our goodbyes as we walked toward the exit.

CHAPTER FORTY-SIX

Zachary

Neither of us said a word during the entire drive home. I held Savannah's hand, intertwining my fingers with hers. It was as if we didn't want to speak, just get to our home and deal with what was consuming us inside.

Gradually, the car slowed down and parked. My door was opened first, I got out, waiting for Savannah to appear by my side.

"What a chilly breeze," she whispered, rubbing her arms.

"Come on, let's go inside." I extended my hand, and we walked together into the house.

The house was quiet; Hazel must have been sleeping with our daughter.

"It's late; Hazel had a long day. She hasn't even slept since she came back from the trip," my wife said, looking around and whispering.

I took a step towards her, stopping right behind, placing my hand on her waist, pulling her close to me, her back touching my chest.

"Damn, Savannah, you make me so proud," I grunted, moving her hair to the side and kissing her neck.

"And what's the reason for this pride?" she asked, closing her eyes and resting her head on my chest as I continued to kiss her.

"The way you defended your husband." Holding her waist, I turned her to face me, lifting her and having her sit on my lap.

"Zachary, my dress is riding up; we could get caught." My wife tried to pull the fabric down, but it was in vain.

"Let me cover it..." With a mischievous smile, I placed my hand on her butt, squeezing it tightly, making her gasp.

"Zach!" Savannah scolded.

"What a great ass." I headed towards the stairs, taking them one step at a time, never stopping kissing her neck.

"What if my sister hears us?" She seemed worried.

"She won't, my love... Even so, just because I want all your moans, let's go to the farthest room." I continued down the hallway, where I was sure Savannah could scream and thrash around without anyone hearing.

I grabbed the doorknob, entered the room, and then locked it. The light curtains allowed the outside lights to illuminate the room. I went to the bed, laid her in the middle of it, stretched my hand to the bedside table, turned on the lamp, and had a clear view of my sweet wife.

"It's like having a mirage right before my eyes..." I removed my jacket.

"Zachary... and if we make love, what will become of us afterward?" she asked, propping herself up on her elbows, looking at me with a crease in her forehead.

"Afterward, we can go to our bedroom and sleep." I gave a small smile, took my shirt out of my pants, and then threw my tie on the floor.

"It's not just that..." She bit the corner of her lip when she saw me unbuttoning my shirt and tossing it on the floor.

"I know you're scared. After everything I've put you through, it's impossible not to be suspicious. But I only ask you to trust me, Savannah. I promise every day of my life to make you the happiest woman," I spoke the purest truth, from the bottom of my heart.

Stopping between her legs, I rested my hand on the bed, covered her body with mine, and brought my face close to hers, biting her lower lip and pulling it back.

"Savannah, will you be mine forever? This time for real? As my wife, my partner, the mother of my daughter, and of my future children?" She lay back on the bed.

Our eyes, one on the other, spoke volumes. Words weren't necessary to understand how our bodies connected from the very first moment we met.

"Yes, Zach, I want to be yours. Even though I'm apprehensive about our future, I want to be entirely yours..."

"Don't be apprehensive, don't be afraid. I promise every day, until the rest of my life, to prove I'm the right man for you."

I slid my hand down her waist, got on my knees, slid down to her feet, and removed her heels. My eyes fixed on her delicate feet.

"Is there anything about you that isn't perfect?" I asked, with a hint of mockery, slowly massaging her toes.

"Senator," Savannah whined, tilting her head back.

"Speak, my sweet Arizona girl." I lowered my lips, kissing her leg, slowly moving up, making sure to kiss every little piece of her skin.

"Your hands make me feel like I'm touching the sky," she whispered with a loud sigh.

I grabbed the hem of her dress, lifting it. My wife raised her arms, and I pulled it over them, leaving her semi-naked. My eyes traveled down her beautiful body.

"Savannah Fitzgerald, stop looking at me with those pleasure-filled eyes." I leaned my body over hers, ran my hand down her back, and unfastened her bra. Savannah wasn't expecting this, so she let out a small squeal, trying to cover her breasts, but I prevented her by holding both her hands. "Don't you dare cover yourself."

Our eyes met amidst my words.

"It's just that it's been so long since we last had sex." She bit her lip anxiously.

"It may have been too long, but I've never forgotten the body of the woman who took over my mind." Gently, I made Savannah lie back down on the bed.

Her long blonde hair spread out, a vision of paradise, her chest rising and falling rapidly. Her swollen nipples, which I couldn't resist touching, I stroked with my thumb until I lowered my face, took them in my mouth, and nursed on them.

I sucked them intensely, sliding my tongue over the sensitive skin of her nipple, listening to Savannah's soft moans of pleasure.

That night she was going to be mine, completely mine. If there was one thing I bitterly regretted in my entire life, it was pushing her away, abandoning her when she needed me the most. If I hadn't been such a jerk, we wouldn't have lost those almost three years. Sadie wouldn't have grown up away from me.

I switched nipples, giving attention to the other one. Her fingers touched my hair, and after years, I let a woman touch me, and damn, what a delicious feeling to have her fingers in my hair, scratching me with her nails...

Like the sweet blooming of a flower, that's how Savannah touched my heart. I was hopelessly in love and completely captivated by that woman.

CHAPTER FORTY-SEVEN

Savannah

I felt his tongue grazing my stomach, moving lower and lower until it touched my intimate spot.

"Zach," I whimpered as my husband's nose brushed against my pussy.

He simply gave it a sniff, as if I were an aphrodisiac perfume.

"How I missed this sweet pussy," he said, opening his mouth and licking the folds of my skin.

"Zachary... oh..." I moaned loudly, unable to contain my instincts.

"Don't hold back, I want to hear all your moans, Savannah. We're far from our daughter's room for this reason..." His voice trailed off as he began to slide his tongue over my pussy with more lust.

My hands touched his hair, splayed my fingers over his silky strands, spreading my legs further, offering Zachary all my intimacy. With all the pleasure that resided within me, I gave myself up completely, my shyness fading away, leaving only the lust of sordid feelings to dominate me.

I pressed his head against my pussy with a bit of force, rubbing it against his mouth, making small movements, craving the friction that overwhelmed me.

"Zachary," I cried out for him, feeling beads of sweat accumulating on my body from all the tension coursing through me.

Moans escaped, my hand gripping his head tighter, not allowing him to say anything.

I tilted my head back, my eyes rolling, biting my lip to keep from screaming and feeling my husband's tongue sliding in all the right places.

"Don't stop... oh... don't stop..." I begged without even realizing it, just feeling the waves of excitement coursing through my body, plunging me off that precipice, like a free fall, with tremors overtaking me.

He knew I was having an orgasm, but he didn't stop, sucking me dry. I eased the grip on his head. I let myself be carried away by that delicious wave of shivers.

With my eyes closed, I smiled lazily as my husband climbed up, covering my body with his.

"Your post-orgasmic expression is so warm, so deliciously exciting." I opened my eyes, seeing his bare chest.

I raised my hand, touched Zachary's defined abdomen, and felt it warm. My husband didn't move my hand, letting me touch him there.

"You talk about me like that, but you're incredibly hot." I smiled mischievously. "And only mine..."

"Completely, entirely, wholly yours." Zachary stood up.

He began to remove his pants, followed by his underwear. My eyes were on him the whole time, savoring the image of having that senator as my husband.

"I want to fuck you with no barriers..." With my legs open, he covered me again. "And I want to come inside you..."

"Zachary," I whispered his name, touching his shoulder.

"But I won't do any of this if you don't want it." His eyes locked with mine.

"Doing this we could have another baby," I murmured, feeling the tip of his extremely hard member touch the tip of my sensitive pussy.

"I want to be a father again, I want to see my wife going through the stages of pregnancy, seeing her get nauseous, arguing with me when she's so pregnant that nothing will make her happy, at least mom was like that when she was pregnant with Scar. I want to hear our baby's first cry, be by your side..." His penis penetrated me as he spoke. "I love you, my sweet Arizona girl, and within me there's no doubt that you are my beloved, the only woman who touched my heart with all this intensity, I love you, Savannah."

I blinked several times, feeling tears welling up in my eyes.

"Throughout our daughter's pregnancy, this is what I dreamed of, you coming to me, telling me how much you loved me, and you didn't come, you weren't there..." A tear rolled down my cheek.

His finger touched that single tear, drying it.

"I'll never forgive myself for this, I will always be flawed with you for this mistake of mine, even if I spend my entire life asking for forgiveness, it won't be enough. But I promise with everything that resides within me, that I will spend every day of my life telling you how much I love you, redeeming myself for our past, a past that cannot be changed but can serve as a lesson to never again push away the woman I am completely crazy about." Zachary's cock slid through my folds, taking me completely.

My eyes closed, and I felt that wonderful mix of pleasure overtaking me once again.

"Now all I need is you, I need your body, only my husband, my senator..." I begged, running my hands over his back, pulling him closer to me.

"Yes, I will be yours forever..."

Zachary began to penetrate me with more force, my nails scratching his back, his hand spread out under my neck, pulling my hair with a bit more force.

"Touch me, Savannah, take me as *yours... your...*" my husband seemed to be pleading in his way of speaking.

It was impossible to stop scratching him; I needed to channel all that frustration into something.

"Zach... oh..." I moaned a bit loudly, our eyes meeting, only the sound of our bodies colliding and echoing in the room.

My husband brought his lips to mine, kissing me urgently, getting lost in our kiss, not separating our bodies.

"Savannah... *I... I...* need to pull out..." he growled, wanting to withdraw his cock.

"No, don't pull out, come inside me, let's expand our family" my voice came out muffled by his lips.

"Fuck, fuck, fuck... how I love you, my sweet Arizona girl" he grunted as I felt the spasms course through my body.

My husband thrust deeply one last time, and I felt his warm jets completely taking over me. His strong body fell on top of mine, our heavy breaths echoing in the room.

My eyes closed, my body sweaty. After a long few seconds, he withdrew from me.

"That... that was amazing" I murmured with a languid body.

"You can say that again... can I ask you something?"

"Yes?"

"Don't tell your sister about our attempt to have a baby, for now." I turned my face to meet his gaze.

"And why wouldn't I?"

"If we succeed, I want to surprise them." Zachary gave a lazy smile.

"I like that." I smiled back.

"Shall we take a shower? I want to wash my wife, and maybe go for a second round of sex..."

"Can you handle a new round?" I asked, making a face.

"My love, I'm years behind on your body" he teased, getting up from the bed and making a move toward me.

A little squeal escaped my mouth when Zach picked me up in his arms and carried me to the bathroom.

CHAPTER FORTY-EIGHT

Savannah

I felt my body being pulled against a strong chest, hands running over my stomach. I opened my eyes, knowing exactly where I was, in my bedroom, mine and his. My husband.

"Zach?" I whispered his name, wanting to know if he was awake.

"*Hmm*..." from his sigh, it was clear he was awake.

"If your intention was to wake me, you succeeded" I murmured, turning with some difficulty as he still held onto my body.

"And was it a stylish awakening?" Our eyes met, and a brief lazy smile appeared on his lips.

"Look, it's not every day I'm woken up like this." My husband's hand slid down my back, pulling me closer to him.

"If this is what being married is like, I feel worse for having missed out on it for almost three years of our lives." His face moved closer to mine.

"It's all your fault." I turned my face to avoid being kissed by him. "Morning breath isn't the best, and this is kind of our honeymoon, you don't need to know right away that I don't smell great in the morning..."

My sentence trailed off as he let out a delightful laugh.

"So, is that where the smell is coming from?"

"Hey." I gave him a light tap on his shoulder. "Do you have to throw it in my face like that?"

"It's a joke." Zachary tried to pull me closer, but I ended up sitting on the bed, escaping from him.

"Deep down, there's a grain of truth in every joke." I frowned, pouting.

"At least this way we can say you have a flaw." My husband also sat up, folding one of his legs, exposing his chest as the blanket slid down.

"Sure, I feel so much better now" I said, obviously playing it up.

Zachary reached out, pulling me by the arm, and I soon straddled him.

"Savannah, you could have the worst breath ever, and I'd still love you, still pull you into my arms, kiss your sweet lips." Holding the fabric of my nightgown, he pulled it up.

"*Hmm*..." I closed my eyes, feeling my body shiver as his hand began to slide over my stomach.

Zachary didn't even seem to mind that I hadn't said I love you yet. I knew I loved that man, but I felt like the moment wasn't right yet.

"Ride my cock, my sweet Arizona girl" he requested, pulling my panties to the side.

Without saying anything, I simply grabbed the waistband of his sweatpants, pulled them down, and freed his extremely hard member. I rubbed my pussy against it, and my husband moved the small fabric of my panties to the side, helping me sit on his cock.

I held onto my husband's shoulders, feeling him fill me completely. I bit my lip a bit forcefully as his hand moved up my back and splayed over my hair, gripping it possessively.

"You're perfect, Savannah" he growled, kissing my neck. "That's it... move deliciously on my cock..."

Not stopping the kisses, I couldn't help but rise and fall on his cock, my wet walls embracing him, as if marking territory that this member was ours.

"Zach... *hmm*..." I whined, gyrating on his cock, and with the hand holding my panties, he squeezed my ass.

"*Mine*... completely mine" he grunted, pulling my hair and holding me tightly.

Last night we had incredibly hot sex in the bathroom, leaving me practically numb, and now we were here, having sex again, and it felt like I was never totally satisfied, as if my body fed off his.

"*Yours*... only yours." With his hand in my hair, Zachary lowered my face, making our eyes meet.

The glow of pleasure shone on him. He brought his lips to mine and kissed me with a bit of aggression, our teeth clashing, each needing the other.

"*I*... *I*... need you" I whispered, my voice breaking from our frantic kiss.

"I'm yours, Savannah. *Only yours*..." he roared.

That made me feel like an amazon, riding Zachary's cock and feeling him fill me completely, droplets of sweat sliding down my body.

I couldn't stop, as if I had a need for it, needing to seek out all my relief, all the desire that was repressed inside me.

"Savannah, my love... *I*..." his voice trailed off as my walls tightened, and my husband thrust hard inside me.

I released, surrendering to the orgasm while Zachary came inside me, his fluid filling me, feeling him slide down my walls. Without getting off him, my husband lay down, pulling me close. I lay on his warm, sweaty chest, Zach's hand releasing my hair and sliding down my back.

"Definitely, morning sex has just made it into my ranking of best fucks" he whispered, making me smile.

"How did we go from arguing about morning breath to almost having wild sex?" I lifted my face to meet my husband's eyes.

"Simple, when we argue, we can forget everything with a good fuck." Without stopping the caresses on my back, Zachary made me shake my head.

"Keep dreaming. This wasn't even a real argument. We're not going to end up in sex every time."

"It would be too good *to* be true." He made me roll my eyes.

"We need to get up. Sadie will come knocking on our door any moment now." Carefully, I got up, removing his cock from inside me, feeling the fluid trickle down my legs, which made him look down.

"I can't wait for us to have another member in this family." My husband's sideways smile made me return it. "Yesterday, when you were already asleep, I checked my phone to see if there was anything important, and I ended up seeing a piece about us..."

"I don't want to know if it's something bad" I murmured, turning around, feeling his hand hold my wrist, pulling me back.

"It wasn't bad, my love, otherwise I wouldn't even mention it. — Zachary's fingers slid down my arms. "The photo is incredible, and right at the entrance of the event, at the moment you blushed when I whispered in your ear, you look stunningly beautiful. That photo had a very positive impact; we're going from the sudden and forced marriage to the most passionate couple of the year. According to some headlines, the wife of the California Senator is completely captivated by his charms. Little do they know, it's me who's captivated by her."

"Is that serious?" I frowned.

"Couldn't be more serious. Check your phone, they're saying wonderful things about my wife." He winked. "Savannah, all I want is your happiness, and I'll do everything I can to make sure everyone in the United States sees what an amazing woman my wife is."

Unable to contain myself, I jumped on top of him, my body covering his.

"Zachary Fitzgerald, I love you, I love you so much that I think it's impossible to love someone this much." That was the moment, I felt in my heart that it was time to reveal my feelings for him.

CHAPTER FORTY-NINE

Zachary

I ended my call with Christopher; we needed to make a few final adjustments to our commercial scripts for a new ad that was going to be made. Since that was something that could be dealt with another day, I chose to work from home today. That way, I'd be closer to my girls.

I put my phone in my pocket, left my room, and descended one step at a time, lowering my eyes and seeing my girl in the living room, or rather, my girls.

Savannah was sitting on the floor while our daughter seemed to be preparing imaginary food. My footsteps were noticed by them. Both of them looked up together.

"Has Hazel left already?" I asked as I approached.

"Yes, she went to college to drop off the last of her enrollment documents and to visit Aunt Natalie" I loved how she called my aunt her aunt, as if we shared all our relatives. "I hope Hazel doesn't run into her cousin; he's always so arrogant."

"In time, you get used to his closed-off demeanor." I shrugged, sitting behind our daughter, running my hand through her blonde hair.

"Me? I don't care about his lack of humor, but the problem is that for some reason, he seems to be bothered by my sister." Savannah lifted her face, looking at me with doubt in her eyes.

"If he does anything to Hazel, please let me know..."

"My sister will never say anything; Hazel is the vengeful type, she'll get revenge on her own." Savannah sighed.

My wife was the type of person who embraced everyone, somehow trying to make everything work for herself and everything around her.

"As for that, only time will give us an answer." I placed my hand on Sadie's waist, lifting her and sitting her on my lap.

"Papa, foo" the little one complained when her imaginary food fell to the ground.

"Oh, look at the mess Daddy made, letting all the food fall on the floor" I said, adding a touch of drama to my voice.

"Wow... wow... wow...." Sadie kept repeating, making me laugh.

My eyes met my wife's, who was watching the whole scene.

"What do you think about us preparing everything again? Can Daddy help us with little Buba's meal?" Buba was the name of Sadie's doll; she called her little Buba.

"I'm considered the best chef in all of California." My wife gave me a curious look. "I'm trained in imaginary cuisine, the same kind our daughter is preparing..."

Savannah shook her head, letting out a loud laugh. I sat on the floor, bringing our daughter along with me.

"Who's going to be the cook?" I asked, lowering my face to Sadie.

She handed me a small pink pot along with a plastic spoon.

"Papa..." Sadie clapped her hands.

"Did Hazel say if she slept well?" I asked, following my daughter's instructions.

"Yes, she said she didn't wake up at all" Savannah replied. "Oh, no, Buba woke up and is starting to cry."

"Oh, no, quick Daddy, quick." My daughter stood up, stamping her little feet on the floor in such a funny way that made me smile, holding back a laugh.

"All done, but we need to blow on the food; it's too hot." I brought my mouth close, pretending to blow, and my little one did the same.

Since she didn't know how to blow properly yet, the sounds came out louder.

Sadie took the pot from my hand, turning to my wife, who placed the doll between her legs, and our daughter knelt down, pretending to feed Buba.

"Only you two could make me play with dolls." I smiled, watching the perfect mother-daughter interaction.

I opened the camera on my phone, capturing the moment in a photo, then opened my *Instagram*, posting the image to my *story*, and that act went unnoticed by Savannah.

My wife seemed more relaxed, more at ease, after she said "I love you" with all the words, reflecting all her love in her gaze.

If there was one thing I had no doubt about in this life, it was my love for Savannah.

She entered my life in the most unusual way, almost getting hit by the car I was in, and our connection was almost immediate. If it weren't for my fears and the demons that haunted me, we might have saved the time we spent apart, loving each other.

Or everything happened in the time it was meant to be; she reemerged in my life like a phoenix, rising from the ashes, bringing along all her good energy, her sweet smiles, the way she carried everything around her.

I knew she was too good for me, but I was also sure that I wouldn't let her slip away from me again.

Savannah was like a ray of sunshine that brightened all my days.

"Zach?" Savannah called me, pulling me out of my daydream. "Is everything okay? You look like you're in another world..."

She pursed her lips, letting her words hang in the air.

"I'm fine, I was just daydreaming." I flashed a big smile. "Thinking about this beautiful family I have."

"Zachary, you're such a fool." She rolled her eyes, starting to blush. "Aren't you going to work today?"

"I am. By the way, I'm heading to the office here at home now; I need to handle some family affairs, have a video conference with William. I can do all of that from here, close to my girls." I got up from the floor, leaning down to give Sadie a kiss on the top of her head.

"Alright, my love." I winked at her, turning and heading towards the stairs.

Savannah knew that, in addition to our political involvement, our family had investments spread across the United States, investments that I could monitor from anywhere. It was a large portfolio that began in my grandparents' time, passed down to my father and uncles, and now was in my hands, along with William, Christopher, and Chris's parents still had the law firm that came from Natalie's family.

I slowly climbed the steps into my newest office, where, if all our efforts paid off, Christopher would win as president, and we would be living in Washington D.C. for a long time.

CHAPTER FIFTY

Savannah

I gently closed the door to my daughter's room. I knew she was peacefully napping.

Holding my phone, I saw a message from Natalie. She informed me that everything was fine with my sister. Hazel had gone to visit the law office where she would be an assistant to Zach's aunt, and she might even intern in the field she was studying.

My sister was very excited about this new opportunity.

Natalie sent me information about one of the events they were starting to adjust. From what I understood, it was a charity ball for a girls' home here in the district. It detailed everything they would be collecting and how the funds would help the institution.

I was very impressed; everything was organized with charts and the names of the contributors, specifically the women behind the charity ball. What impressed me most was seeing my name among those women, as if Natalie already knew I would agree.

She was waiting for my response and really wanted to know if I would accept. Obviously, without thinking twice, I would love to be involved in helping. If there was something I was good at, it was helping others.

I replied to Natalie, went back to my messages, and also responded to my mother. We spoke every day because she wanted to know how I was adapting to my new life.

Would it be strange to say I was born for this? That I felt complete and strangely fulfilled?

I approached the door to Zachary's office; it was slightly ajar, so I pushed it open gently. I peeked inside, seeing him lift his eyes toward the entrance.

"Did Sadie sleep?" He wanted to know.

"Yes, she's sleeping like a little angel." I smiled as I entered the office. Zachary closed his laptop with a sweep of his hand.

"Come here, my Arizona girl." I approached him, taking his hand.

"How come I didn't see you take that photo earlier today?" I asked after seeing his *stories*.

"Simple, I was too focused on the challenging task of getting Buba to eat." He pulled me onto his lap, placing one leg on each side.

"Don't even get me started on how difficult that is..." My sentence trailed off when he picked up a tie from the desk. "What are you going to do with that?"

"Nothing," even as he denied it, a mischievous smile sparkled on his lips.

"Zachary..."

He grabbed both of my wrists and moved them to my back.

"I wanted to remind you of a day... the day I had you tied up." I didn't move my hands, allowing him to bind me.

"Which day was that again?" I feigned ignorance dramatically.

"The day my heart decided to love you, and my cock chose to fuck you," he teased, bringing his lips close to mine, kissing me and pulling back with a bite.

"Oh... surely Sacramento will be marked as the city of our most bizarre experiences." I bit the corner of my lip, rubbing my dress slowly against his erect penis that was pressing against the fabric of his pants.

Without warning, he quickly got me on my feet, turned my body, and made me bend over the desk in his office, with my butt sticking out for him. With my hands bound behind my back, I turned my face to the side.

"My love" I declared, alarmed.

"I love it when you call me your love." He smiled to the side, unbuttoning his pants and lowering them to free his penis.

"I love loving you, my senator." I smiled, closing my eyes as his hand lifted my dress, pushing it up.

He pulled down my panties while using his other hand to caress my butt.

"Ah!" I let out a little scream as he smacked my butt with some force.

"Hot!!!" He groaned, brushing his penis against it, sliding down to my pussy, which was already fully ready for him.

My husband pressed his cock into my folds, starting slowly, filling me completely. He pulled out and entered me again with slow movements, and I bit my lip.

"My bound hands make me anxious," I whined.

"Your anxious expression turns me on even more," he declared, leaning over my body.

Sliding his hand underneath me, he released my breast, squeezing my nipple with some force as uncontrolled moans began escaping my mouth.

"Oh... heavens..." I whimpered.

"Yes, moan for me, my delicious wife, give me all your moans..." he roared, making me roll my eyes.

Zachary tormented me for long seconds, pinching my nipples, fucking me slowly, until he straightened up and gripped my ass tightly. He began to penetrate me with great intensity, his pelvis crashing into my butt.

Moans escaped my lips; it felt good, incredibly good. Only our heavy breathing filled the space.

I felt my walls constricting, he grunted loudly, thrusting one last time and coming deeply. His body leaned over mine, and we stayed like that for long seconds.

Slowly, he got up, and with my husband's help, I turned around. Zachary held my waist, sitting me on top of his desk. With that movement, the panties that were around my ankle fell to the floor. He untied the tie, and our eyes met.

"I love you, my senator," I whispered, raising my hand to touch his face.

"I love you, my Arizona girl." His lips touched mine slowly, a gentle and slow kiss.

"Can I boast about being one of the few who can touch you?" I smiled as he bent down, pulling up his pants.

"You can boast about many things, about having my heart, about being the only one my body chose to let touch. I lived for years without letting anyone touch me, and now I want you to caress me all the time."

Zachary proved to know how to love me unconditionally; he proved he could be the best husband and the best father our family could have.

He was my husband, the only man who touched me, who loved me with that crazy yet delicious intensity. Even though we had been apart for almost three years, when we reunited, it felt like there had been no distance. It was as if we had always been there, side by side.

There was no more room for doubt or any other obstacle that could harm us.

Amidst many misunderstandings, intrigues, mistakes, and wounded pride, we decided to give ourselves that new chance.

EPILOGUE ONE

Savannah

One Month Later...

Sadie was running across the lawn, a beautiful smile on her face, so perfect, my little one. The light blue dress made her look like a princess.

My mother-in-law had arrived a week earlier, along with my father-in-law, to start preparations for Sadie's second birthday. This was going to be the first celebration with my husband's family.

Grace was considering the possibility of moving to Washington D.C., with the intention of being closer to her granddaughter. She said that Scar was very focused on her studies and no longer cared about family, so there was nothing keeping her in Sacramento.

I felt someone's hand at my waist and turned around, smiling as I saw my mother.

"I'm so happy Dad agreed to fly," I told her.

"After he nearly scared a flight attendant to death, we arrived safe and sound. — She shook her head, unable to hide her smile. — And when we got to the airport and he said the flight was fine, that he'd take another hundred trips, honestly, your father is a case study."

My parents had arrived the night before, and everyone was staying at our house. There was no reason they shouldn't be; the house was huge, easily accommodating our family.

"Mom, that man is quite a case," I teased affectionately.

"Grandma... Grandma" my little one saw my mother talking to me and called her.

"I'm going to be with my little one." Mom stepped away to be with her granddaughter.

Everything was ready: inflatable toys, tables scattered around the backyard of my house. The princess-themed decoration was perfect. We were just waiting for the guests.

"Where is your head at?" Hazel appeared beside me.

"Can you believe our little girl is turning two?" I said, somewhat melancholic.

"And that soon we'll have another little thing running around this house?" My sister made me look at her.

"Did you manage to buy Sadie's onesie?" I asked, seeing her nod.

"I'm dying to see everyone's reaction, especially the senator's." Hazel gave a sly smile.

Zachary had asked me not to tell my sister about our attempt, but Hazel is my sister and best friend, it would have been impossible to hide something like that from her, especially since we always shared everything.

From the very beginning, Hazel knew we weren't being careful, obviously Zachary didn't know that, after all, my sister was helping me with the surprise revelation. I waited until I was sure I was really pregnant. We needed Natalie's help, and my husband thought I was attending one of the charity ball meetings we were preparing when, in fact, I was at a clinic getting a beta HCG test to confirm the pregnancy.

Aunt Natalie also knew about the pregnancy and was very happy with the news.

"After we sing happy birthday to Sadie and everyone has cake, we'll change her and have her walk to her father wearing the 'promoted to big sister' onesie" I whispered the plan to my sister.

"Perfect." Hazel looked back with a grimace. "Here comes the world's owner, the untouchable man, the king of arrogance, the very epitome of pride, the..."

"Wow, Hazel." I widened my eyes, knowing who she was talking about, though I was still surprised by the amount of praise.

"What's the point of being a complete hottie if, when he opens his mouth to speak, only crap comes out? And that's because he barely talks to me; if I weren't so grateful to the Fitzgeralds, I'd be campaigning against this jerk," my sister finished the sentence, grumbling.

"Oh, please, don't make such a fuss."

"Can you believe he went to the office yesterday and snubbed an intern just because she had drafted a document incorrectly? Does Mr. Perfect never make mistakes in his life?"

"Hazel." I bit my lip, wishing she would stop talking as I saw Christopher stop behind her, listening to her complaints.

"Miss Bellingham." My sister's eyes widened as she was caught red-handed.

"I tried to warn you," I whispered.

"I'm the only Bellingham now, aren't I?" Hazel murmured back to me, turning around and lifting her face to look at Christopher.

"Should I be concerned about you taking family business outside the office?" My husband's cousin had that ever-arrogant tone of voice.

"Technically, Sav is a Fitzgerald, I didn't do anything wrong," Hazel quickly composed herself, shrugging her shoulders.

"Always with a sassy comeback," Christopher retorted.

"Maybe the problem is with you, thinking everyone should bow down to the almighty Christopher, the melancholic and lonely one." I bit my lip, lowering my face but unable to control a smile at what my sister had called him.

"I still don't understand what my mother sees in you," he said irritably.

"Bitter people don't understand happy people, don't worry, Mr. Fitzgerald, it will pass." Christopher sighed deeply, turned, and left, leaving me alone with Hazel again.

I lifted my face, seeing my sister muttering low curses.

"I'm absolutely sure that all this bitterness comes from a lack of sex. I wonder if his hand is calloused from all the masturbation he must be doing..."

"Oh my God! Hazel! My husband's cousin's sex life is none of my business!" I reprimanded my sister.

"Hazel, he doesn't have sex, and since he became a widower, he hasn't been practicing anymore." Hazel widened her eyes again as if this was something from another world.

"Look, I really don't want to have these kinds of thoughts about Christopher." I gave a big smile, looking at the man walking away with his cell phone to his ear. "But it's quite a waste, we both have to agree."

"Too much, I'd play at that amusement park until I was exhausted." She sighed, making me roll my eyes, but still smiling.

I WAS STILL RECOVERING from the birthday song; the pregnancy hormones were starting to affect me. I cried buckets, recalling the first two years of my daughter's life. How hard it was, but luckily I had a great family support system.

I was happy to see Michael there; fortunately, Zach's jealousy eased a bit when he found out that Michael and Olivia were engaged and had set a wedding date. I was simply thrilled with that news. All I wanted was my friends' happiness.

Sadie had gone inside with Hazel; my sister was going to change her so she would come back wearing the surprise onesie.

I felt Zachary's fingers interlace with mine.

"Why do I feel like you're acting strange? Did something happen? Should I be worried?" My husband wanted to know.

"I'm fine, my love, I never thought I'd be so well accepted in something." I smiled.

"Although it wasn't quite like that in the beginning." A sideways smile also appeared on his lips.

He was referring to the sensationalist sites which, thank God, had stopped bothering me. After we became the couple of the year, it seemed that good news about people didn't get much attention, so it gradually stopped. They had nothing more to say about me. We proved in various ways how real our love was.

When I saw Hazel letting Sadie out in front of our house, my heart raced. We were in front of the decoration table for my daughter, my eyes on Sadie, which made my husband look at her too.

"Why did you change her clothes? The dress was so beautiful," Zachary said, unable to see our daughter's outfit clearly.

"She wants to play with the toys..."

My sentence trailed off as Sadie approached us, my husband's eyes focusing on the outfit she was wearing. I saw the exact moment Zach's eyes lit up, tears welling up in that beautiful blue.

"Is this for real?" Zachary asked, bending down when our daughter stopped in front of him.

"Yes," I whispered, placing my hand on my belly, feeling the tears start to fall from my eyes again.

"You're pregnant?" My husband looked at me with affection, and I just nodded, unable to contain myself.

Soon everyone around us noticed the surprise and came to us, but before they got close, Zachary took a step towards me, pulling me into his arms, hugging us three, or rather four, with the new member of the family inside me.

"We're going to grow, our family is going to grow, I'll be able to see every stage of your pregnancy. I love you, Savannah, I love you dearly." Zach whispered, taking a step back with a quick kiss on my lips.

Soon everyone was congratulating us, and all I could do at that moment was cry, cry with emotion, with joy.

That was my place in the family, with Zachary, with my little Sadie, and with the people most important to me.

I found my place in the world, and it was with the most unexpected person. How I loved loving Zachary Fitzgerald.

EPILOGUE TWO

Zachary

Six years later...

"Papa." I lowered my gaze from the notebook, a spontaneous smile spreading across my lips.

"Come to daddy." I turned in the chair with the wheels moving.

Jayden's chubby and unsteady little legs were coming towards me. It had been only a few weeks since he had learned to walk. My son approached, I bent down, picked him up, and sat him on my lap.

"Where is your mom?" I asked curiously.

On days when I didn't have any personal matters to attend to in Parliament, I stayed at home, working and being with my children.

"Down" that was his way of saying that mom was downstairs.

"And how did you get up here..."

"Jay" at that moment, Sadie's breathless voice burst into my office. "Damn, kid, how did you get here so fast? Mommy can't know about this."

Sadie placed her hand on her heart in her best dramatic fashion.

"What were you doing that made you lose sight of your brother?" I raised an eyebrow suspiciously.

"Nothing, dad." She shook her head as she entered my office, about to grab my son.

"Nothing at all?" I asked again, knowing that those blue eyes always tried to win me over with a sly smile, and most of the time, she succeeded.

"Maybe, but only maybe, I got distracted watching a video on my phone." There was that sly smile that made me soften.

"Can we make a deal?" Sadie nodded. "When you're with Jayden, no distractions, okay?"

"Yes, daddy, I promise it won't happen again." I winked at her. "Can we not tell mommy about this?"

"Tell her what, exactly?" At that moment, Savannah walked into my office.

"Oh... damn" Sadie tried to smile at her mother, but that act didn't work as well with her mom as it did with me.

"Sadie?" My wife wanted to know.

"Sorry, mom, I said I wouldn't get distracted, and that's what happened." She gave that guilty look; my eldest daughter really did apologize when she did something wrong; she wasn't the type of child who just spoke without meaning it.

Sadie had recently turned eight; she was an intelligent girl, one of the top students in her class, our pride, and she loved her siblings more than anything. It was she who asked to be with Jay, wanting him to accompany her in almost everything.

"You're forgiven; I believe your father has already told you, but I'll repeat it: no distractions when you're with your brother..."

"I'M HERE, FAMILY." The shout made everyone wince; the little girl burst into my office.

"Sis." Jayden jumped off my lap, running clumsily towards his sister.

Alexis was the vibrant spirit of our home and had the loudest voice. I wonder what I did for my daughter to come with all the traits of her aunts, as if she had inherited a bit from Scarlett and Hazel. Even their own children weren't as similar to them.

"Come on, Alex, watch your manners," Sadie complained.

"Today's gymnastics class was so cool; look at what I learned to do." She first hugged her little brother tightly, making him complain, but soon after, they both started laughing.

Alexis had her golden hair in a ponytail; she was the only one of our three children with green eyes. She loved gymnastics, channeling all her excess energy into her favorite sport.

My middle daughter lifted one of her legs to her head, balancing on the floor with just one. I bit my lip at the sight; her flexibility sometimes amazed me.

"How cool." Sadie quickly started clapping.

"Can I teach you? Want to?" Alexis suggested.

"Oh, definitely not. I don't want to turn into a stretchy woman." My eldest daughter began shaking her head numerous times.

"I'm going to change…"

"Take a shower first," Savannah requested.

"Okay, mom." Just as flamboyantly as she had entered, she left.

"Can I take Jay with me?" Sadie asked.

"Yes, but pay attention to him," my wife advised.

Sadie nodded, taking Jayden's little hand, and walked out. My two daughters studied in the morning, but on some days they spent more time in extracurricular activities.

"Someone could have warned us that we'd have three kids with completely different personalities," my wife said. "Although it wouldn't have changed anything; I wouldn't give up any of them."

Savannah was one of the influential women in high society, having become a major reference in such a short time, always in charge of all the NGOs, participating in charity meetings organized by the women's club.

And on top of that, she was actively involved in the lives of our three children. I sometimes wondered how she managed to handle it all.

I opened my legs, let her settle between them, and holding her waist, I brought my head close to her belly, embracing her and inhaling her delightful scent, my daily calm.

"A lot to handle?" she asked, stroking my hair.

"Who said the second term is easier than the first?" I inquired, somewhat mockingly.

We were in Christopher's second term; my cousin had managed to win the presidential election for a second time. He was elected one of the youngest presidents the United States had ever had.

"Are you thinking of running for president when Christopher's term ends?" she asked, which was something we talked about every day.

Christopher couldn't be re-elected to the presidency after his second term, and my name was one of the most talked-about in the spotlight.

"That's my life goal," I told my wife, lifting my eyes to hers.

"I'll love being the First Lady of the United States." I pulled Savannah onto my lap.

"Are you ready to see our whirlwind Alexis shouting in the White House?" I brought my lips close to hers.

"Wherever my family is, I will be." Her fingers brushed my cheek.

She was the woman I fell in love with every day. Savannah was up for anything, holding my hand and making everything real. She never faltered. And the woman I thought was weak was the strongest I had ever known.

If I ever wronged anyone, it was her. Savannah always surprised me, being the most incredible woman anyone could have by their side.

There was no doubt; Savannah was born to be mine, and I was born to be hers. My wife, the only woman my heart chose to love, and touch every day.

"To the White House," I murmured, embracing her, knowing we were about to take another big step, and with my eyes closed, knowing that I had the best family a future presidential candidate could have.

THE END...

Did you love *Shattered by Secrets*? Then you should read *Whirlwind of Desire* by Amara Holt!

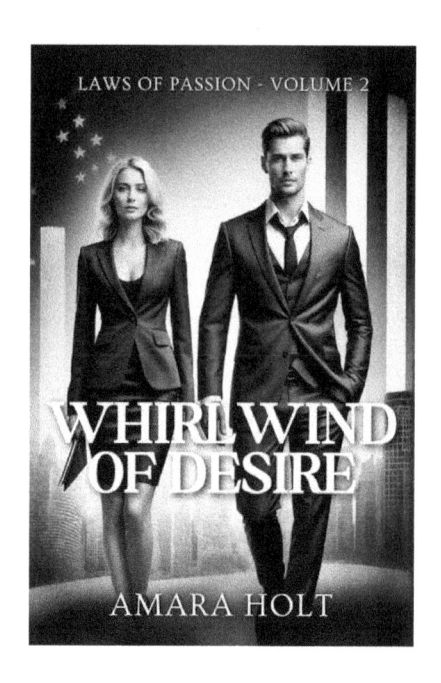

Whirlwind of Desire is a gripping romance that brings together **passion**, **power**, and **forbidden** love. William, a calculating and ambitious governor, has his life meticulously mapped out—until Zoey, the wild, unpredictable sister of his best friend, storms into his world. Zoey has dreamed of being with William since childhood, but to him, she's always been **untouchable**. Now, fate throws them together, and the lines between **duty** and **desire** blur.

As Zoey makes her boldest move yet, she never expects the fallout—**rejection** and an unexpected **pregnancy** with the man she's loved her whole life. William, torn between his **political career** and his feelings for Zoey, is faced with an impossible choice. Will he protect his heart, or surrender to the **whirlwind** of emotions that threaten to upend his carefully built life?

Whirlwind of Desire is a must-read for fans of **steamy, slow-burn romance**, packed with tension, drama, and the intoxicating allure of **forbidden love**. Dive into a world where passion overpowers reason, and discover what happens when love defies all expectations.

About the Author

Amara Holt is a storyteller whose novels immerse readers in a whirlwind of suspense, action, romance and adventure. With a keen eye for detail and a talent for crafting intricate plots, Amara captivates her audience with every twist and turn. Her compelling characters and atmospheric settings transport readers to thrilling worlds where danger lurks around every corner.